P.C. HA

C. Hawke
Mysteries

THE
PHANTOM OF
86th STREET

P.C. HAWKE
mysteries

THE PHANTOM OF 86th STREET

- - - - - - - - - - - -

PAUL ZINDEL

Hyperion
New York

Volo and the Volo colophon are trademarks of Disney Enterprises, Inc. All rights reserved. No part of this book may be reproduced or transmitted in any form or by any means, electronic or mechanical, including photocopying, recording, or by any information storage and retrieval system, without written permission from the publisher. For information address Volo Books, 114 Fifth Avenue, New York, New York 10011-5690.

Printed in the United States of America
First Edition
1 3 5 7 9 10 8 6 4 2

The text for this book is set in Janson Text 11.5/15.
Photo of thunderstorm: Don Farrall

Library of Congress Catalog Card Number on file.
ISBN 0-7868-1591-4
Visit www.volobooks.com

Contents

THE PHANTOM OF 86TH STREET • Case #8

Case #8 began something like this:

On the way to school early one spring morning, I came to a complete standstill as the New York Post headline caught my eye: PHANTOM STALKS 86TH STREET BUS! Later on, in homeroom, I read the story aloud to my best friend and fellow detective, Mackenzie Riggs.

Mr. Rubén Baio, a janitor who had just come off the graveyard shift at Presbyterian Hospital, had been mysteriously murdered on the 86th Street crosstown bus. According to the driver, the bus ride had been without incident. One by one, his passengers had gotten off, until only Mr. Baio, who appeared to be sleeping, remained. But when they got to the last stop, the driver discovered that Mr. Baio was not sleeping. He was dead. Someone had slipped a scalpel through his ribs and punctured his heart, then disappeared like a phantom.

After I finished reading, the kids in our homeroom started razzing Mackenzie and me about how we were going to drop out of school to go meddle in murder cases and drive the police nuts. Just because we'd been involved in a few cases, everyone at Westside School acted like they thought Mac and I spent 24/7 wandering around the city, looking for corpses. Yes, it's true that I'm the only kid at school whose laptop's home page is nypoliceblotter.com, but that doesn't mean I'm obsessed. Besides, Mackenzie and I agreed to leave this one to the authorities—finals were coming up, and the police could handle it.

At that point, there was no way we could have known that in a few short days we'd become so deeply

involved in the case that we'd be riding a death
bus with a homicidal maniac trying to make
phantoms out of us.

Recording the truth, the whole truth, and
nothing but, I am

C. C. Hawke

(a.k.a. Peter Christopher Hawke)

1

Beethoven, Brie, and Bloodshed

You could tell spring had come to New York because the nights were warming up, the tulips on Park Avenue had blossomed, and the squirrels were jumping through the tree branches like preschoolers at a piñata party.

As Mackenzie and I picked our way through the crowd gathered on the Great Lawn of Central Park, I started serenading her in my best country-and-western twang. "You may have been my springtime girl, but I was just your fall guy."

"P.C., that's got to be about the lamest song I've ever heard," said Mac. "And besides, you're a native New Yorker. You can't sing country."

"Can't, or shouldn't?" I asked.

"Both. Now shut up and look for someplace to sit. The concert's going to start any minute."

Mackenzie and I looked around for any unoccupied territory where we could spread out our blanket and crack open our picnic basket. But it was the New York Philharmonic playing Beethoven's greatest hits—a special, pre-season concert in the park. It was jam-packed.

Finally, Mac spotted a tiny patch of grass between two large extended-family type groups. We squeezed ourselves into our spot, spread the blanket, and sat down.

"I got eggplant baba ganoush, tabouli, olives," Mac said, unpacking the little pint tubs. "Garlic toast, sun-dried tomatoes, *bocconcini*—"

"Oh, man, I love those." *Bocconcini* are these incredible little marinated fresh mozzarella balls. I reached over and stabbed one with my fork. Mackenzie gave me a disgusted you're-a-greedy-*bocconcini*-hog look and kept pulling out containers.

The Philharmonic was tuning up. The timpani boomed. The violins and cellos ran up and down their scales. I chomped, swallowed, and said, "Music outside always sounds better. Why is that?"

Before Mackenzie could answer, a toddler from the family on our right Frankenstein-walked over to us, and plopped into my lap. His mother came chasing after him. "Come here, you little rascal!" She scooped him up, apologized, and carried him back to their blanket. I could hear him shrieking with laughter over the music.

"Want a drumstick?" Mac asked, popping a pita triangle loaded with hummus into her mouth.

"No thanks."

"I got the fried chicken specially for you."

Mackenzie is an exceptional vegetarian. That means she makes exceptions.

"Thanks, but I kind of lost my appetite." I lay back and looked up at the sky. It was still light.

"Isn't this nice?" Mackenzie said after a while.

"I guess. Though it stinks that you can never see any stars in this lousy city."

"Is something bothering you, P.C.?"

"No," I said. "What would be bothering me?"

"I don't know. It's just that you don't seem to be enjoying the concert very much, and—"

"I'm fine, okay?" I interrupted her. "Just because I'm not hungry, and I'd like to see more than half a dozen measly stars every once in a while, doesn't mean anything's wrong with me."

"Okay," said Mac. "I was just asking. You seem down."

"I'm not *down*," I insisted. "I'm just not *up*. Is that a crime?"

After a few seconds of cold silence, I sat up and looked at Mackenzie. I could see she was ticked off and was about to apologize when we heard the blare of sirens over on Fifth Avenue. The flashing red-white-and-blue lights of police cars and ambulances came to a screeching halt just a few blocks south of where we sat.

"Let's check it out," I said, getting to my feet and tossing forks, knives, and napkins into the basket.

"Don't you want to stay and listen?" Mackenzie asked. "They're going to do the Ninth Symphony at the end of the night. Your favorite!"

"Nah," I said. "You heard one symphony you heard

'em all." I popped the tops back on the olives and *bocconcini* and tossed them in the basket.

"Don't just throw things in there, P.C.!" she said. "You're making a mess."

"I'm in a hurry." I took a chomp out of a chicken leg. Suddenly my appetite was back. "This is something big. I've seen at least eight cruisers and half a dozen ambulances."

We raced out of the park and onto Fifth Avenue, lugging the picnic basket. With my free hand I gnawed on the chicken leg, waving it at slowpokes who failed to clear the sidewalk fast enough.

"P.C., you almost clobbered that little old lady back there," Mackenzie scolded me.

"Didn't even come close," I said, tossing the cleaned drumstick in a garbage can. "Wow! Look what we have here."

We slowed down as we approached the Eighty-fifth Street exit. The blindingly bright red ambulance lights strobed the intersection. There were about half a dozen cop cars on the scene. Not to mention the taxi, a white van, and a late-model Honda that were strewn about the intersection. Steam poured from the taxi's hood, which was crunched in practically to the windshield. The van was halfway up on the sidewalk of the uptown side of Fifth, facing downtown. Across the street from the van, the Honda was wrapped around a lamppost.

Inside the open back of one of the ambulances, a

medic was taking the pulse of a middle-aged lady with a bandage on her forehead. We could hear her saying, "I didn't see her! She darted out of nowhere! The next thing I knew . . ."

"Come on," I said, tugging on the picnic basket. Mackenzie followed.

We forced our way through the crowd that had gathered on the corner and saw the body of a woman lying facedown on the curb. From the unnatural position of her arms—palms up, right hand flung across the small of her back—it was obvious she'd been hit at great speed. A paramedic was kneeling over her, but she was dead.

"What happened?" I asked the heavyset guy in a Mets cap who was standing next to me.

"Don't know, buddy," he said. "She got whacked by the taxi, I think."

A man in a blue nylon NYPD jacket pushed through the crowd and hollered at us. "Show's over. Go home, before I run you down to the station for loitering."

A uniformed cop came over and said, "Lieutenant Douglas, we got all the entrances to the middle section of the park closed."

"Thank you, sergeant," said the lieutenant. He shook his head. "Nutcases ought to be in Bellevue, not out on the street where they can hurt themselves. Ran screaming straight into traffic and ate a bumper. Guess it's what the voices told her to do."

Most of the crowd had dispersed by now. But Mackenzie and I knew that the lieutenant had better things to do than arrest anybody for loitering. So we stuck around, to see what we could see. After a few minutes, the paramedic guy who'd been examining the dead woman wandered over to a nearby ambulance.

"Here's our chance," I said to Mac. "Drop the basket, and let's take a closer look."

We put the picnic basket in the doorway of an apartment building, then walked casually over to the body. I knelt down to take a better look at her. Since she was facedown, it was hard to tell how old she was. She had long, straight brown hair, and she was wearing a stone-washed denim jacket and blue jeans.

"Take a look at this, Mac," I said. She knelt down next to me. "Cuts on the back of her neck—you can see them through her hair." I really wanted to brush her hair out of the way to take a better look, but I didn't want to disturb any evidence.

"Her jacket is slashed too," Mac said, pointing to several cuts that ran from just below the collar down between her shoulder blades to about midway down her back.

"Looks like she was mauled by a saber-toothed tiger," I muttered.

"Those are some pretty strange marks to be on someone who was hit by a car."

I nodded. "Exactly what I was thinking."

Just then the paramedic guy returned. "Hey, kids, move along. You don't want to look at her. You'll get nightmares."

"We've seen worse," I assured him. And it was true, we had seen worse—far worse. Mackenzie's mom, the city's chief coroner, had let us accompany her to her job at the city morgue.

"Sure you have, kid," said the paramedic, draping a long sheet over the body. "Sure you have."

It wasn't worth it to argue with the guy.

We wandered over to where a small group of people had been herded by several cops. I overheard the cop in the nylon jacket—Lieutenant Douglas—tell a sergeant to take down the names of all the witnesses and not to let any of them leave.

"Hey, officer," said a wiry woman in spandex who was straddling a racing bike, "I gotta be in Chinatown in half an hour. Can we get this over with?"

Lieutenant Douglas ignored her, and went on questioning an elderly Asian man.

I went up to spandex-bicycle woman. "Rough night, huh?"

"No kidding," she said. "I was just coming out of my building here when all hell broke loose."

Mackenzie asked, "Did you see what happened?"

"Sure, I saw what happened," she said. "This lady—the dead one—got off the bus with her boyfriend. I was putting my helmet on, and I saw them walk down the sidewalk a ways. The next thing I know, she's screaming her head off and running into traffic. Then, *wham! Pow!* She's bouncing off cars like a pinball."

"Did you get a look at the boyfriend?" I asked.

"Nah," she answered. "He was wearing a jacket with the hood up. Couldn't see his face."

"How'd you know he was her boyfriend?" Mackenzie asked.

"He was walking next to her like he was her boyfriend. The funny thing is, though, he split after she got hit by the car. You'd think he'd stick around to see if she was okay. Jeez!"

I nodded. "Yeah, you would think that—*if* he really was her boyfriend."

"Thanks for the info," said Mac.

"Sure thing."

We scanned the group of witnesses waiting to be interviewed by the cops. The Asian guy had disappeared, and Lieutenant Douglas was now talking to a matronly lady with a vicious-looking Pekinese tucked inside her fur-trimmed coat. The rat-dog snarled and snapped at anything that came within four feet of him.

Nearby, a very tall, very thin man wearing a red-black-and-green knit hat was yelling into a cell phone. "It wasn't my fault, man!" he said. "Insurance will cover the damages. . . . Yeah, man . . . Okay, okay."

I waited till he hung up, then walked up to him.

"You the driver?" I asked, pointing to the taxi, which was still emitting steam gustily.

"My cab, yes," he said.

"Can you tell me what happened?"

He looked surprised. "You're young to be a policeman, little man."

I smiled and shook my head. "Not a cop. Just an interested civilian."

The man smiled back. "If you say so."

"So what did you see?"

"Not much, man. It happened so fast. I was going south on Fifth, just dropped off a fare at Eighty-eighth Street. All of a sudden this woman, this crazy woman, she just jumped in front of my car. Crazy expression on her face—huge eyes. Like she'd seen a ghost, you know?"

"Or a phantom," I said.

"Yeah, man, a phantom. She was coming right at my windshield. I slammed on the brakes and closed my eyes. Then I heard a big *whap*, like the sound of a cricket bat smacking a side of beef, you know?"

"Sure, sure," I said, though honestly I was having a hard time imagining it.

"Ooh, it was terrible."

The poor cabbie looked like he was on the verge of tears. I patted him on the shoulder and said, "It wasn't your fault. There was nothing you could have done."

"Thanks, man."

I looked around at the crowd of witnesses, onlookers, and cops and grabbed Mackenzie by the arm. "Mac! We have to stop him!"

"Who?"

"Follow me!" We ran over to where Lieutenant Douglas was motioning to the paramedic guy to take away the body of the woman. A small circle of uniformed cops was standing around the lieutenant. A walkie-talkie crackled loudly. One of the cops was saying, "So then my no-good brother-in-law—"

"Lieutenant!" I shouted, bursting into the circle of cops.

"What do you think you're doing, buddy?" the cop asked as I tried to get the lieutenant's attention.

"I need to talk to—"

"Move along," the cop said, slapping his nightstick against the palm of his hand. "We're busy here." He turned and said to one of the other cops, "So anyway, my wife gave the lazy bum two hundred—"

"But—" I started up, and the cop faced me again.

"Listen, pal—" he said, poking me in the solar plexus with the butt end of his nightstick. At that moment, Lieutenant Douglas stepped between us and said, "Cool your jets, Hansley."

The cop muttered "Punk" under his breath and turned back to his buddies.

Lieutenant Douglas turned to me. "Okay, kid. What do you want?"

"Those people over there are trampling a crime scene," I said.

The lieutenant shook his head. "There's no crime scene here. This was an accident."

"It was homicide," I insisted. "I'm sure of it."

The lieutenant looked at me like I was nuts. "What's your name?" he asked.

"P.C. Hawke," I said. "This is my friend Mackenzie Riggs."

Mackenzie stepped up and flashed her thousand-watt smile. "Lieutenant Douglas?" she said, reading the badge clipped to his breast pocket. "Lieutenant Howard Douglas?"

"Yes," said the lieutenant, surprised that Mackenzie knew his first name. Heck, *I* was surprised Mac knew his first name.

"My mom's mentioned you more than once," Mac gushed. "She's chief medical examiner for the city—Kim Riggs. You've heard of her, haven't you?"

"Sure, sure."

"Because she's certainly heard of you. She thought your work on the Papaya King shooting was first-rate."

Lieutenant Douglas struggled not to grin like a monkey. Unsuccessfully. "Did she?"

"Oh, yes. 'First-rate investigative work. A top-notch detective.' Those were her words exactly."

"Well, what can I do for you, Mackenzie? And your friend P.T.?"

"*P.C.*," I corrected him.

"P.C.," he repeated. "Okay. Tell me why you think this was a homicide."

"The dead woman wasn't crazy or high or suicidal," I said. "She was trying to escape an attacker."

Mackenzie continued, "We talked to some people who saw her get off the bus with a man—who has now mysteriously disappeared. And she had cuts on her neck and back that looked like knife slashes."

"*And* there was another murder on this bus route just three days ago," I said. "It was in the *Post*—the Phantom of Eighty-sixth Street, remember?"

Lieutenant Douglas paused. After a few seconds, a lightbulb clicked on in his head. "Officer Hansley," he said. "Clear this intersection and tape off the area around the body. Call forensics and get them down here pronto. We've got a murder on our hands."

"Thanks for listening, Lieutenant," Mackenzie said.

"Just trying to do a first-rate job," he said. "And hey, thanks for your help, Mackenzie, P.C."

"No problem."

"And say hello to your mother for me, okay, Mackenzie?"

"For sure," Mac said.

He wandered away, barking orders at the cops who were swarming the area with a new sense of purpose.

I turned to Mackenzie. "Wow! What a coincidence, your mom knowing the lieutenant."

"Don't be an idiot, P.C.," she said. "I've never heard of him before. While you were having your macho showdown with Officer Nightstick, I asked another cop about the lieutenant. He told me about the Papaya King case and gave me the lieutenant's first name. The rest was people skills."

"You mean flattery, deceit, and manipulation."

Mackenzie tucked her long blond hair behind her ears and smiled. "If that's what you want to call it."

"Humph." I had to admit to myself that Mac's method was more effective than my burst-in-yelling technique. I didn't have to admit that to her, though. "It's been a long night," I said. "Let's go home."

2

Be Courteous to Your Coroner

The next day after school Mackenzie and I paid a visit to the Central Park precinct on the Eighty-sixth Street Transverse.

Mackenzie, playing both sides against the middle, had told her mom about meeting Lieutenant Douglas the night before. In her version of the conversation, it was Lieutenant Douglas who'd expressed admiration for her mom's work. So Mrs. Riggs had been happy to give the lieutenant a call, asking him to cut Mac and me some slack. The lieutenant was more than happy to oblige.

Lieutenant Douglas led us into his office. "I want to thank you kids again for your help last night."

"Have you identified the victim yet?" Mac asked.

"Yes." He handed her a file. "Name was Amanda Griffith, twenty-seven years old. Single, no kids. Nurse at Presbyterian Hospital on the Upper West Side. She was on her way home when the incident happened."

"Did you track down her boyfriend?" I asked. "The one who disappeared?"

The lieutenant shook his head and took a long slug

from his oversize coffee cup. "She had an on-again, off-again boyfriend out on Long Island. But his alibi checked out. He was clocked in at his job managing a dairy plant when Amanda was killed."

"So who was the guy who got off the bus with her?" Mackenzie asked.

Lieutenant Douglas shrugged. "The bus driver told us that Miss Griffith got on the bus alone and sat by herself. His statement's in the file."

Mac flipped through some papers.

"My guess is the killer waited until Amanda exited the back of the bus, then followed her," said the lieutenant.

"Did anybody else see a man with Amanda?" I asked.

"We talked to a homeless man who was camped in the woods by the museum." The lieutenant slurped some more coffee. "He claims he saw a woman get off the bus, followed by someone in a hooded jacket. He heard tires squealing, and several seconds after that, the person in the hooded jacket ran by him into the woods."

"Did he get a look at the person's face?"

"No, it was too dark," said the lieutenant. "He was a bit of a character, this homeless guy." He held his finger up to the side of his head and drew circles in the air.

"What about the cuts on Amanda's neck and back?" Mackenzie asked.

"Looks like they were made by some kind of tool. Like a hacksaw."

"How bizarre," I said.

"We don't know it was a hacksaw," the lieutenant cautioned. "Only that it was some kind of bladed instrument with very fine teeth. Could have been a medical saw."

"A medical saw?" Mackenzie said. "That ties in with the murder last week—the guy who got the scalpel in the heart."

"I suppose," he said.

"Maybe the killer works in a hospital," said Mackenzie. "Or maybe a medical-supply company."

"Or he could be a doctor," I suggested. "Many experts believe that Jack the Ripper was a physician, you know."

The lieutenant held up his hand. "Hold on. At this point it's not even clear we're dealing with a single murderer, much less a serial killer. The two cases could be unrelated—and the bus thing could be a coincidence."

The phone on his desk rang. "Douglas," he answered.

While the lieutenant took his call, Mackanzie and I looked over the file. Even though the lieutenant was still not convinced that we were dealing with a serial killer, I noticed that he'd included information from the Baio murder in the Amanda Griffith file.

"Listen to this, Mac," I said. "Rubén Baio worked as an orderly at Presbyterian—the same hospital Amanda Griffith worked at."

"That can't be coincidence."

Lieutenant Douglas hung up the phone and said, "I've got a meeting to go to now."

"Have you checked on the Presbyterian connection yet?" I asked.

"We're getting around to it," he said, grabbing his coffee cup. "See you later, kids."

We walked with him out of his office, and he took off down a hallway.

"Are you thinking what I'm thinking?" Mac asked.

"To Presbyterian?"

"To Presbyterian," she confirmed.

Half an hour later, we emerged from the subway at Broadway and 103rd Street. A panhandler asked us for change. I dug in my pockets and gave him a dollar bill.

"Double or nothing says I can tell you where you got them shoes," he said, pointing at my feet.

I was wearing Nike sneaks—shoes you could buy at about a thousand stores in Manhattan alone. I'd gotten my pair at a basement dive on St. Mark's Place in the Village. There was no way the guy'd be able to guess that.

"Okay, shoot," I said. "Where?"

"You got 'em on your feet," he said, and held out his palm.

"Gotcha," Mackenzie said to me.

Feeling like I'd just fallen off the back of a turnip truck, I handed the guy another dollar.

"Much obliged, brother," he said. Then he turned and called to a passerby, "Hey, lady, bet you five bucks I can tell you where you got them shoes."

"What a scam," I said to Mackenzie as we crossed Broadway.

Presbyterian Hospital is a massive seven-story brick pile that takes up an entire city block. The red bricks are stained almost completely black from decades of exposure to bus fumes, soot, and general New York City grime. As we walked up the steps to the front entrance, I noticed a pair of stone gargoyles leering at me from above the doorway.

We walked into the main lobby. The all-too-familiar, unpleasant hospital smell of pine disinfectant, rubbing alcohol, and disease hit me in the face. Suddenly I felt tired and headachy. "Maybe it's just the weird Hogwarts exterior," I said, "but this place gives me the creeps."

"We'll make it quick," Mackenzie promised. "Come on, there's the information desk."

A woman with elaborate hair extensions and gold fingernails that were a good five inches long sat reading a magazine behind a high counter.

"Could you tell us where Amanda Griffith worked?" Mac asked the woman.

Without looking up, she answered, "Fifth floor. Oncology."

Then Mackenzie asked where Rubén Baio worked.

"Fifth floor. Oncology," came the answer again.

Mac and I exchanged a look. Not only did the two victims work at the same hospital, they even worked in the same department.

"Coincidence, Dr. Watson? I think not," said Mac in a fake English accent as we headed toward the elevator.

"Let's just go up there, see what we can find out, and get out of here, okay?" I said.

Mackenzie dropped the imaginary pipe she was holding and said, "Sure, P.C.," in her normal voice. We rode the elevator in silence and got out on the fifth floor. As we walked to the nurses' station in the middle of the floor, we passed a room marked CAUTION—RADIATION. I flashed back to the times I had watched my mother go through a door like that at St. Luke's. It was a couple of years ago, but I could still remember her smiling at my dad and me, and telling us not to worry.

Mackenzie took my hand. "Are you okay, P.C.?"

I swallowed. I hated crying in front of people. Even Mackenzie, and she was my best friend in the world. "I'm fine," I said. "Let's go."

"Can I help you?" came a loud, nasal voice from across the room. It belonged to a short bleached blonde in a pink nurse's outfit. Her name tag read BRINI THOMPSON.

We introduced ourselves, and explained that we were investigating the deaths of Rubén Baio and Amanda Griffith.

"Had either of them received any threats that you were aware of?" I asked.

"Omigod!" said Brini. "I don't know about Rubén. We weren't close. He wasn't my type. All he talked about were his dogs. He bred pit bulls, you know?"

"No, we weren't aware," Mackenzie said.

"I didn't like him *or* his dogs one little bit. I'm not saying he deserved to die, of course. Omigod, no! I'm just saying I didn't like him."

"What about Amanda Griffith?" I asked. "Did you know her well?"

"Oh!" Brini gave a little cry. "Poor Amanda!"

"She was your friend?" Mackenzie asked.

Her eyes welled up with tears. "We'd been friends ever since she transferred out of ICU three years ago. She was going to be one of my bridesmaids." Brini flashed her engagement ring at us. "Three carats," she said.

"It's beautiful," Mackenzie said.

Brini beamed.

"Was there anyone who might have had it in for Amanda or Rubén?" Mackenzie asked. "Any troublemakers with a grudge against the hospital staff?"

"Omigod," Brini exclaimed. "Listen, honey, hospitals get all kinds. Everyone winds up here sooner or later."

I couldn't help wincing at that statement.

"Oncology's not so bad, though," Brini went on. "I used to work the ER. Night shift. Drug addicts, gangbangers, prostitutes. Guy came in one time with a big iron rivet sticking out of his head. Just walked in off the street. Said his buddy at the building site accidentally shot him with the rivet gun. He felt fine, just needed the rivet pulled out, and could someone turn down the music—he was tired of listening to Donna Summer."

Brini took a deep breath and went on. "There was no music! It was all in his head! Anyway, we pull the rivet out, bandage him up, and are about to send him to neurology when he says, 'Can you put the rivet back in? Now I hear the BeeGees!'"

"That's very interesting," Mac said, "but—"

"You want to know about Amanda," said Brini. "Okay. There was this one creep last fall. His name was Jim Nichols, in for an appendectomy, so he wasn't on this floor. I don't know how he even met Amanda. He saw her around, though, and decided he had a thing for her. Asked her out."

"Did she go?" Mackenzie said.

"No way, honey! Amanda could smell a rat from a mile away. He bought her a dozen roses. She said no. Two dozen. Three dozen. Finally Amanda agrees to have dinner with him, just to get him off her back. Big mistake. Big, *big* mistake. He starts calling her at home, leaving messages, hanging around the floor. Stalking her! One time I asked him to leave, and he wouldn't. Rubén Baio had to—Omigod!"

"What?" I asked.

"It was *Rubén* who threw that nutjob out of here. They almost got into a fistfight in the lobby. Amanda had to file a restraining order against him. You don't think . . ."

Brini looked scared. In a small voice she said, "Well, that's about it. After the restraining order, I never saw him again. But last month Amanda told me that someone had broken into her apartment. The thief had gone through her clothes and smashed a vase—the same vase that Jim had sent the flowers in. Creepy, huh? The police took a report, but they don't really care about things like that. You gotta have a knife sticking in you before they'll do anything."

"Can I see the computer file on Jim Nichols?" I asked. "We'd like to talk to him."

"Sorry, can't let you do that," Brini said. "The law says we have to protect our patients' privacy." She cocked her head, as if she suddenly heard something. "What's that? Someone calling me? I have to go now." She started walking down the hall. "I can't give you permission to look in the computer. Of course, with nobody at the nurses' station, I'd have no way of knowing if you did." Just before she rounded a corner, she called back, "Hit control-P for a list of patients."

As soon as she disappeared, Mackenzie and I scurried to the terminal at the nurses' station and hit control-P. A record for Nichols, James G. popped up right away: in the hospital for three days in November. Appendectomy. No complications. Lives on Eighty-eighth Street. Works at Bransford & Hill Publishers, 777 Fifth Avenue.

I jotted down the information. We'd just cleared out

of the station when another nurse came down the hallway. Her name tag read JEANNIE CLOSE, HEAD NURSE.

Nurse Close had a face like a hatchet and a personality to match. "What are you doing here?" she demanded. "Are you here to see a patient?"

"No, ma'am," said Mackenzie.

We explained, politely, that we were helping the police investigate the deaths of two of her staff.

"Why haven't the police come by here?" Nurse Close slapped her bony hand on the counter of the nurses' station. "I want the killer caught, and I want him caught now! The very *idea* of a psycho maniac killer running around loose! Did you see this morning's paper?"

We nodded.

"The *Post* is calling him the Phantom of Eighty-sixth Street! It's outrageous. My staff is terrified."

"Do you have any idea who might want to—"

"Do I have any ideas?" she said, cutting me off. "I know who killed Amanda and Rubén. It was Willy Corbin. Worked in the basement as a custodial engineer. Janitor, that means."

"Why do you think—"

"Not think, *know*! Poor Amanda, God rest her soul, caught him going through a patient's purse a couple of months ago. She reported the incident to me. When I asked around, it turned out others had observed Mr. Corbin up to no good. Pharmaceuticals gone missing

25

on his shift. Patients reporting stolen cell phones. Petty theft. The man's a criminal, I tell you!"

"Can we talk to him?" I asked.

"If you can find him!" Nurse Close snorted. "He was fired three weeks ago. Amanda testified against him in a personnel hearing. So did Rubén Baio—he'd seen Corbin at the loading dock putting boxes into the back of a van."

"Really. Did the hospital press charges?" Mackenzie asked.

"No. Management decided he wasn't worth the trouble. Firing him solved the problem—so they thought! I heard the police did pay him a visit at his apartment, though. They found thousands of dollars' worth of supplies, toilet paper, soap, stuff like that."

"Sounds like he's a thief," I said. "But that doesn't make him a murderer. You really think Willy Corbin could be dangerous?"

"I don't *think* so, I *know* so," she thundered. "Let me show you something." She ushered us around the counter of the nurses' station and sat in front of the computer. Luckily, Mac and I had remembered to exit from Jim Nichols's patient file a few minutes before.

"Someone's been sending us threatening e-mails," she said. "Take a look at this."

On the screen a message read:

```
You are makeing a BIG mistak. Youl be
```

```
sorry. Im going to get you if its the
last thing i do. Watch your back.
```

"That was from two weeks ago," said Nurse Close.

"What's the return address?" I asked.

"We can't tell. Whoever sent it routed it through a series of phony accounts. It's untraceable. We've gotten others. They're all untraceable. And they get weirder."

She called up another one, dated only five days before:

```
You think your so smart Im going to get
you yet. Ill feed you your childrn and
then kill you for fun. im going to
dance on your dead body and use your
skul for a doorstop. your as good as
dead.
```

"That's disgusting," Mackenzie said. "Whoever sent it must be really disturbed."

"And a lousy speller," I added.

"Willy Corbin dropped out after eighth grade," said Nurse Close. "I'd be surprised if he could spell his name."

I asked her for Willy Corbin's home address. To our surprise, she agreed. Apparently, the rules protecting patients' privacy didn't extend to former employees. Or if they did, Nurse Close chose to ignore them. "He lives in Queens, near LaGuardia Airport," Nurse Close said.

"Norton Avenue, number eleven twenty-one, apartment forty-three."

We thanked Nurse Close for her help. "You kids be careful," she said.

"Don't worry," Mackenzie said. "We'll be okay. And we'll find the killer, too."

Out on the street, I whipped out my cell phone and speed-dialed my friend Jesus Lopez. Jesus is a world-class computer jockey. There's not a firewall in the world that he can't hack through—though he doesn't like the term *hacker*. He prefers "information retrieval engineer."

"Whassup?" Jesus asked.

"Just hanging," I said. "Listen, I want you to do me a favor."

"Does it involve the violation of any FCC regulations?"

I laughed. "Not this time. Everything I need will be in the public record. But if you want to go the extra mile, get creative . . ."

"Say no more. Understood. What do want?"

"I need you to check out any legal complaints filed against Presbyterian Hospital over the last twelve months. Especially anything that hit the courts or the police blotter."

"No prob. I'll get right on it, P.C."

"Thanks, Jesus. You the man."

I hung up and stashed the cell phone back in my knapsack, then turned to Mackenzie. While I'd been talking to Jesus, she'd been window-shopping a pair of thigh-high black leather boots in a boutique window.

"Ever want to write a novel?" I asked her.

"Not really," she said. "How do you think those would look on me?"

"They're perfect for sleuthing. Not."

Mackenzie laughed and turned away from the window. "Now, what did you say about a novel?"

"You'd better think up a good one quick. We're going to try to sell one to James Nichols."

3

The Art of Fiction

The lobby of the Bransford & Hill Publishers building was decorated with a cheesy collection of oversize book posters. Staring down from one wall was a bunch of wind-blown ladies dressed in Victoria's Secret–type outfits swooning in the arms of long-haired lunks under titles like *The Pirate King*, *Passion Under the Stars*, and *All for Lust*. The wall opposite featured sunsets, cattle, cactuses, and titles like *Shootout at Lazy Arrow Ranch*, *Along the Dangerous Trail*, and *The Lonely Riders*. On the third wall were posters for children's books: *The Happy Little Raincloud*, *Buster's Big Birthday*, and *Scruffy, the Cat Who Played Guitar*.

"It's like a sociologist's Ph.D. thesis waiting to happen," Mackenzie observed.

I grunted. I was busy scanning the names of the company's board of directors, which was posted next to the elevator banks, along with a listing of Bransford & Hill departments. Aha! I found a good one: Livingston R. Wendsworth III.

"You remember dear Uncle Livingston, don't you?" I said.

"Oh, certainly, dahling," Mackenzie said in her best Thurston Howell III from *Gilligan's Island* manner. "Summering in Kennebunkport! Wintering in Aspen! Or was it Switzerland?"

"Oh, Switzerland! Aspen simply *swarms* with little people. It's simply *ghastly* now!"

"Frightfully ghastly!" Mackenzie exploded with laughter, and I cracked up too.

"Seriously though," I said, recovering. "We're Livingston Wendsworth's niece and nephew, okay?"

"Got it."

After taking a few deep breaths to clear ourselves of any lingering giggles, we walked up to the receptionist and explained that we had an appointment to see James Nichols.

"Names?"

"I'm Trevor Wendsworth, and this is my sister Sloane," I said.

As the receptionist punched in Nichols's extension, Mackenzie kicked me in the shins. It was all I could do to keep a straight face. Mac, in her black-and-yellow honeybee miniskirt, pink bowling shirt with PINBUSTERS embroidered over the pocket, and black satin choker with a real scorpion encased in Lucite, was about as far from being a Sloane Wendsworth as it was possible to be.

The receptionist turned to us. "Mr. Nichols's assistant says he doesn't have a record of an appointment for you at this time."

"Really?" I said, feigning surprise. "That's strange. Our uncle, Livingston Wendsworth, set up the meeting with Mr. Nichols. We came all the way down from Newport for the day. Mummy will be so disappointed with Uncle Livvie."

"Just a moment." The receptionist repeated this information into the phone. A pause for a few seconds. Then: "Mr. Nichols said go on up, he'll fit you in. Twelfth floor."

When we reached the twelfth floor, a rail-thin guy in hornrim glasses and a yellow bow tie greeted us at the reception area. "I'm Jonathan Mathers, Mr. Nichols's assistant."

"Trevor Wendsworth," I said, shaking his hand.

Mackenzie stepped forward. "And I'm Sloane."

"I see." Mathers shot us a suspicious look, then shrugged and handed us a recent Bransford & Hill catalog. "Wait here. Mr. Nichols will be with you shortly."

We flipped through the catalog—which consisted mainly of celebrity bios, self-help guides, techno-thrillers, westerns, and romances—and tried to think up a good story to sell to Mr. Nichols. I stopped at a page featuring a biography of Shakespeare. A lightbulb went off in my head. "Mackenzie, do you remember *Hamlet* from English class last year? 'The play's the thing. . . .'"

"'Wherein I'll catch the conscience of the king,'" Mac finished. "P.C., you're a genius!"

I was about to agree with her when Jonathan Mathers

came back. "This way," he said, leading us through a confusing maze of cubicles and offices to James Nichols's office. He opened the door and ushered us in. "Trevor and Sloane Wendsworth to see you, sir."

Even though he was sitting behind his desk, we could see that James Nichols was a big guy, with huge shoulders and thick, hairy forearms. He had bushy eyebrows and tufts of hair that shot upward from the sides of his forehead.

Nichols lifted his lip in what I think he thought would pass for a friendly smile. "Have a seat," he said.

Mackenzie and I plopped ourselves into the two cracked vinyl chairs in front of his desk and looked around. Not surprisingly, books and manuscripts were piled everywhere. What *was* surprising was the collection of weapons, of all different sizes and shapes— samurai swords, nunchakus, throwing stars, even a battle-ax. I couldn't help wondering which of the knives here would match up with the wounds on Amanda Griffith's back. "Hobby of yours?" I asked.

"You could say that," Nichols said. He leaned toward us. "So—your uncle must have forgotten to tell us that you two were coming in today."

"That's perfectly all right," Mackenzie said. "Uncle Livvie is so forgetful."

"Now, what can I do for you kids?

"We have a book idea." I turned to Mac. "Sloane, tell Mr. Nichols about our book idea."

Mackenzie gave me a look that said, I'll get you later. Then she said, "Okay. It's a thriller. Set in a hospital— kind of a *Fatal Attraction* meets *One Flew Over the Cuckoo's Nest* thing."

"Ummm-hmmm," said Nichols. He picked up a throwing star and started fiddling with it, turning it over and over in his fingers. It's a good thing Mackenzie was doing the book pitch, because I was mesmerized by Nichols's casual playing around with a deadly weapon.

"It's about a girl, Anna Griffin, who works as a nurse on the mental ward of a hospital," Mac said, really getting into it now. "One of patients—he's there for a minor procedure, a hernia—sees Anna and falls in love with her. He's a TV producer, kind of a big shot, but he has a mean streak. He collects Nazi memorabilia, has a bunch of rifles and helmets and things in his office. Anyway, he asks Anna out a few times but she turns him down. He starts stalking her."

"This is where it gets thrilling," I put in. "Stalkers are scary, don't you think?"

Nichols nodded, but didn't say anything. He started chucking the star down on the edge of his desk and prying it loose, over and over again.

Mackenzie gulped, then went on. "So he starts hanging around the mental ward, till finally they have him thrown off the floor. Anna gets a restraining order, but then someone breaks into her house and goes through her stuff. Creepy, huh?"

"Yes," said Nichols coldly. His dark-brown eyes drilled into Mackenzie. "Very."

"We've done some research into hospitals to make sure we get the setting right," I said. "Have you ever spent much time in a hospital, Mr. Nichols?"

"Can't say I have," he answered, training his laser-beam eyes on me. I had the feeling that he wanted to leap across his desk and bludgeon me with a bo.

Before he could do anything, though, the door opened and his assistant, Jonathan, peeked in. "What is it?" Nichols barked.

"Production says we won't be getting the galleys back on *Delta Commandos* until Thursday. We'll have to push the pub date back a week."

"What!" Nichols exploded, bolting out of his chair. "Didn't I tell you two weeks ago that we *had* to make that date? What kind of idiots are you people?"

"I'm sorry, Jim, but—"

"Don't give me any excuses!" Nichols snapped. "I want those galleys on my desk *tomorrow*, not Thursday, or heads will roll—starting with yours. Now get out of my office. And next time knock before sticking your snout in here, do you understand?"

"Yes, sir," Jonathan croaked. He shut the door.

Mackenzie and I looked at each other. We'd "caught the conscience" of the editor, all right. He was a full-blown psycho.

Nichols sat down again. "Listen, kids, your story

sounds . . . interesting . . . but I'd have to read it. Can you leave me a sample chapter?"

"Um, we don't actually happen to have it here with us at the moment," I said sheepishly. "Maybe we could e-mail it to you?"

"Fine." Nichols got up and came around the desk. He was taller than I'd thought.

I automatically stood up too, and as I did so I accidentally knocked some papers off his desk onto the floor at Mackenzie's feet.

"Oops, sorry," I said. "Could you get those, Mac?"

"Mac?" Nichols said. "I thought your name was Sloane."

"Uh, it is," Mackenzie said. "Trevor sometimes calls me Mac. It's my middle name."

"Short for MacDougal," I added helpfully.

Nichols grunted. It was clear the interview was over. It was also clear that Nichols was as suspicious of us as we were of him. But since he didn't know for sure we *weren't* related to Livingston Wendsworth III, he couldn't do anything about it.

He tried out his smile again and held out his hand. "Trevor, Sloane. Good luck."

We shook. I noticed he squeezed my hand a little more forcefully than was strictly necessary. Then we booked it out of there. Out on the street again, Mac let loose.

"What kind of crazy move was that, P.C.," she said,

"putting me on the spot with that bibliophilic loon up there?"

"You did great, Mac," I said. "Or should I say *Sloane*?"

"And what was with the *MacDougal*?" she shouted. "What kind of goofy name is that? Why couldn't you have just told him Mackenzie? What difference would it have made?"

"Just playing it safe. Didn't want him to know anything about you. Anyway, your book pitch was fantastic. I would've bought the film rights. You had me eating out of the palm of your hand."

"Humph," Mackenzie humphed. "I always have *you* eating out of the palm of my hand. It's not *you* I was worried about. It was Mr. Bizzarro Ninja Stalker Creepoid."

"We'll never see him again—at least not without police backup."

"Even so," Mac said, "I oughta—" She balled up her fist and made like she was going to slug me when my cell phone rang.

"Saved by the bell."

Busy as a Funeral-Home Fan in July

"Whatcha got, Jesus?" I asked, holding the phone to Mackenzie's ear so she could listen in too.

"I searched the public court records and found all legal complaints against Presbyterian Hospital going back two years."

"Cool. I only asked for one year."

"As long as I was there, I figured what the heck. Anyway, there were ninety-four complaints, ranging from food poisoning in the hospital cafeteria to an animal-rights case when the ER refused to admit some joker's pet iguana."

"How many involved oncology?" I asked. "That's where both our victims worked."

"Only two," Jesus said. "The relative of a patient claimed his credit cards were stolen out of his wallet.

"Stolen credit cards, eh?" I said. "Doesn't sound like the sort of thing that would send a person into a frenzy of murderous revenge. Who's number two?"

"A woman claimed hospital negligence contributed to the suffering and death of her mother."

An icy wave hit me in the stomach. Mackenzie gave me a quick sideways look, then said, "Go on, Jesus."

"The plaintiff was one Meredith Claiborne, age thirty-seven," Jesus said. "Senior Analyst at Manheim, Dobbs Securities, on Wall Street."

"I guess that rules her out," I said.

"Why's that, P.C.?" Jesus asked.

"Female, middle-aged. Holds a job in management at a respectable Wall Street firm. Doesn't fit the profile of a serial killer."

"If you say so . . ." said Jesus doubtfully.

"I have an instinct about this sort of thing," I said. "Listen, do me another favor, will you?"

"Shoot, bro'."

"See what you can dig up on Willy Corbin. He was a janitor at Presbyterian before he got fired for stealing. Lives in Queens. We think he may have sent threatening e-mails to the hospital."

"Anything else?"

"Check on James Nichols. He's a book editor at Bransford & Hill. Martial-arts freak. The second victim, Amanda Griffith, had a restraining order out on him. See if you can turn up anything else on him, okay?"

"No prob. Talk to you later, dude."

"Ciao," I said, and punched the end-call button.

Mackenzie asked, "Why are you so sure it wasn't Meredith Claiborne?"

"Intuition," I said.

"That's funny?" she said. "*My* intuition tells me that Meredith Claiborne has a very strong motive. We should check her out."

"No," I said. "It wasn't her. I'm sure of it."

Mackenzie raised her eyebrows.

"Let's drop it, okay?" I said.

"Sure, P.C. We can drop it. For now."

The next day we decided to walk the route the Eighty-sixth Street bus takes across Central Park. Having grown up on the Upper West Side, we'd taken that bus a million times. But until you have a reason to really pay attention to something—such as when you're investigating a murder—it's surprising how much you don't bother to notice. For instance, neither Mackenzie nor I could remember how many stops the bus made in Central Park itself.

The answer, it turned out, was only one. About midway across the park a single streetlamp hung over a bus stop. On the north side of the street were the woods and trails of the park. On the south side was a small police kiosk, not much bigger than an old-fashioned phone booth.

We walked up to the kiosk and tapped on the glass door.

"Whatcha want?" said the officer inside, setting down the crossword puzzle he was doing. "Lost? The skating rink is that way," he said, pointing. "The rose garden is that way."

"We're not lost, officer," I said. "We're helping Lieutenant Douglas on the Rubén Baio and Amanda Griffith cases."

After a quick call to the lieutenant, the policeman introduced himself as Officer Jamison and said, "What can I do for you?"

"Is there an officer stationed here round-the-clock?" Mackenzie asked.

"You bet," said Officer Jamison. "We take six-hour shifts, in groups of two. My partner's patrolling the area around the pond and castle right now. This is our home base. You'll find someone here twenty-four hours a day."

"Did the officer on duty see anything strange on the nights that Baio and Griffith were killed?" I asked.

"I'm not sure about Griffith," Officer Jamison said, "but I was on duty the night Baio was murdered."

"And?" Mac said.

"Well, a guy did get out at the stop here around eleven o'clock," said Officer Jamison.

"What did the man look like?" I asked.

"Couldn't really say. It was dark, of course, even with the streetlamp. And he was wearing a hood."

"Just like the man who was seen following Amanda Griffith," I pointed out.

Officer Jamison nodded. "Yeah. Kind of a coincidence, isn't it?"

We thanked Officer Jamison for talking with us, and headed down toward the Conservatory Pond, one of our favorite spots in the park. After stopping for some ice cream, Mackenzie and I found an empty bench facing the water and watched while a balding guy with a potbelly tried to interest his toddler son in the intricacies of tacking against the wind. The kid was having none of it, being far more interested in an anthill.

"I think we should talk to Willy Corbin," I said.

"Sounds good," Mackenzie said, sucking a drop of melted ice cream from the bottom of her cone. "We should probably check out Meredith Claiborne, too."

"I don't see why," I said. "She's already been eliminated as a suspect."

"Not by me she hasn't."

"Look, the killer's got to be a man," I argued. "The person who followed Amanda Griffith was a *guy*. The person who got off the crosstown bus in the middle of the park the night Rubén Baio was killed was a *guy*. It couldn't have been Meredith Claiborne."

"We don't know anything about her, other than where she works," Mackenzie pointed out. "Also, everyone just *assumed* that the person in the hooded sweatshirt was a man, but nobody's actually seen his face. With the hood up, how can you tell for sure if it was a man or a woman? Especially in the dark?"

"I can tell a man from a woman," I said. "Even in the dark, even in a hooded sweatshirt."

I could tell Mac was getting annoyed with me. She snapped, "I think there are other reasons why you don't want to interview Meredith. And that's fine. But I don't think *we* should write her off as a suspect."

I didn't say anything.

"Maybe I should talk to her alone," Mackenzie said.

I took a deep breath. "No, you're right. She is a suspect. I'll come with you."

Mackenzie squeezed my hand. We sat in silence for a minute. The bald guy steered his yacht around the pond. His son poked a stick into the anthill.

Mac offered me a lick of her ice-cream cone. "Want some? It's good."

"No thanks," I said. At the moment I had no appetite for anything.

After school the next day, Mackenzie and I were on our way to Sal's for after-school nosh when Jesus called and gave us the update on Willy Corbin.

"I hacked into Presbyterian's server, but all I was able to find was a copy of his dismissal," he said. "And I couldn't find any criminal record. I'll keep working on it."

"Good. If there's something out there, you'll track it down."

"Track it down, shoot it, stuff it, and mount it in the parlor, my friend."

"Remind me never to try to hide anything from you.

Jesus laughed. "Likewise, Sherlock."

"Anything else on Corbin?"

"Turns out there is an e-mail account registered at his address. I haven't been able to figure out yet if he sent the e-mails to the hospital—whoever did it knows a thing or two about covering his tracks. But I'll crack it eventually."

Mackenzie took the phone. "Hi, Jesus. Have you gotten anything on James Nichols?"

"Nothing yet, I'll keep looking."

"Thanks, Jesus," said Mackenzie. "Listen, come over to dinner in a couple of days, okay? My dad's making moussaka."

"I'm there. Later."

"Later," we both said, and hung up.

Sal's was crowded, but Mac and I managed to find a spot next to some kids from Westside. Between bites of a spicy pepperoni-and-onion slice, Mackenzie said, "I need to go down to Wall Street this afternoon. There's a used bookstore down there, Alvie's, that specializes in chess books. Dad's birthday is coming up and I wanted to get something on the Sicilian Dragon defense for him."

"What about the Strand?" I asked, naming the huge bookstore on Broadway in the Village. "It's a lot closer than Wall Street, and I can go to Forbidden Planet while you're perusing chess books."

Mac took a gulp of her Coke and said, "I think I'd rather go to Alvie's. The clerks there will be able to help me pick out a good one."

I could always tell when Mackenzie had an ulterior motive. I waited a beat.

"And hey, while we're down there, we can drop in on Meredith Claiborne. Mannheim, Dobbs is just down the block from Alvie's. Two birds with one stone."

Bingo! "I see what you're doing, Mac," I said. "And it's okay. Let's check out Meredith. You don't have to pretend to be looking for a chess book for your dad to get me to go."

Mackenzie smiled. "Thanks, P.C. Dad hates chess."

I whipped out the old cell phone again and, a few minutes later, was on the line with Meredith Claiborne's executive assistant.

"My name is P.C. Hawke," I said. "My friend Mackenzie Riggs and I are on assignment from *Shred*, the lifestyles magazine for today's fly youth. . . . Oh, you've never heard of it? You will, believe me. Anyway, Mackenzie and I have been assigned to do a piece on women financial leaders, and we were given Meredith Claiborne's name. The article's going to bed tomorrow morning, so it's urgent that we meet with her this afternoon. . . . I see. Yes, I'll hold."

"'*Shred*, the lifestyle magazine for today's fly youth'?" Mackenzie said, laughing. "Where'd you come up with that one?"

I winked at her. "The catacombs of my unconscious," I said, using her dad's psychologist-speak.

Linda came back on the line, and told me Meredith

would fit us in at four. I looked at my watch. We'd have just enough time to make it.

"We'll be there," I said, and hung up.

After a quick jaunt on the number 4 express train to Wall Street, we found the Mannheim, Dobbs building. Whatever it was they did, the company took its security seriously. An armed guard stood discreetly in the corner of the reception area, staring into space. We zipped up to the forty-first floor where Meredith Claiborne had her office.

Meredith's executive assistant, Linda, met us in the lobby. "Meredith is honored that you'll be including her in the article," she said. "What was the name of your magazine again?"

"*Shred*," I said.

"The lifestyle magazine for today's fly youth," Mackenzie added helpfully.

"It's new," I told Linda. "Condé Nast is behind us, though."

"Condé Nast," Linda repeated. "Really?" She seemed impressed—Condé Nast is the company that owns *Vogue*, *GQ*, and a ton of other high-end rags.

Linda showed us to Meredith's office, which had banks of floor-to-ceiling windows that took up two whole walls, and a giant mahogany desk that was the size of a 1974 Lincoln Continental. Sitting behind the desk in an eight-hundred-dollar Aeron chair was our quarry: Meredith Claiborne herself. Her magenta power suit clashed sickeningly with her cherry-red complexion, which got darker and darker as she yelled into her wireless headset and typed in short, machine-gun bursts on one of her three Power Macs. As we walked in, she yanked off the headset and threw it on her desk, nearly knocking over a glass of champagne.

"You've got eighteen minutes, kids. I'm expecting a call from Kuala Lumpur."

Mac took out a notebook and pen and started jotting down notes while I started in with the questions. "I understand you've been involved in some major business deals, Ms. Claiborne." Actually, I had no idea what it was, exactly, that Meredith did at Mannheim, Dobbs Securities, but it gave her an opening to talk about herself. Anyone who was willing to be interviewed by a magazine for today's fly youth had to be a major publicity hound.

"Yes, well, I did just engineer the merger of Kittredge Industries and Halfmark Limited," she said. And she was off and running. For the next fourteen minutes, she went on to name other companies she'd either merged or broken up. All the while, Mac sat scribbling furiously. As Meredith continued raving, flinging around numbers in dollars, euros, and yen, I took at quick peek at what Mackenzie was writing. It was a list of CDs she wanted to buy.

Mercifully, Linda came into the office with a champagne bottle and refilled Meredith's glass, interrupting her soliloquy just as my eyes were about to glaze over and Mac was about to run out of CDs. "The party's in full swing downstairs," Linda said to Meredith.

"I'll be right there," said Meredith, draining her grass. "Wouldn't want old Charlie to retire without saying good-bye to him. By the way, Linda, did you get that fax through to Zurich?"

"Yes, they got it this morning."

"Good. Now about the party I'm giving next Friday. I've decided to have it at my apartment rather than at the Four Seasons. Make sure my Damatsu clients receive invitations. Also Paul Wells at WestTel and Regina Kearns of Kearns, Slaughter."

"Will that be all?" Linda asked.

"More champagne, please." She held out her glass, and Linda filled it to the brim. "Thank you, Linda."

When Linda left the office, Meredith checked her watch and said, "Three minutes. What else would you like to know? Would you like to hear how I got my start in business?"

"Actually, I was wondering if you just got back from vacation," Mackenzie said.

Meredith looked annoyed. "I don't have time for vacations. Do you think I've gotten as far as I have by lounging around the Caribbean?"

"Well, you look like you have a sunburn. . . ." Mac said.

Meredith took out a compact and examined herself.

"Oh, this? It's not sunburn. It's just a slight allergic reaction to alcohol, nothing serious. Doesn't stop me from drinking with the guys. . . ." She leaned toward Mackenzie. "I'll tell you a little secret: it's still a man's world, you know. If you want to make it in business, you have to be one of the boys."

Mackenzie raised her eyebrows. "Oh? Should I put that in the article?"

Before Meredith could respond, a tinny electronic rendition of the *William Tell* Overture—or, as most people know it, the old *Lone Ranger* theme—sounded.

Meredith glanced down at the miniature beeper attached to the belt of her power suit. "That'll be Kuala Lumpur. That's it, interview's over. Now I expect you to fax me the article before you print it. Here's my card," she said, handing it to Mackenzie. "Call if you need any more information."

As I stood to shake hands, I saw that the screen saver on one of her computers was a photo of Meredith with her arms around an older woman with gray hair propped up in a hospital bed. From the resemblance, it was obviously Meredith's mother. I tried to think up a tactful way of bringing up the lawsuit Meredith had filed against the hospital, but Linda came in and ushered us through the security door and into the reception area. The guard in the corner continued to stare off blankly into the middle distance.

When we were out on the sidewalk again, Mackenzie

said, "So, do you feel like checking out Alvie's? I don't need to buy anything, but it might be fun anyway."

"The chess shop? Sure, why not?"

On the way we stopped and bought Italian ices from a tiny hole-in-the-wall shop. The shop was literally a hole in the wall—a window set at waist height into the building's facade. A heavyset Italian lady, complete with black dress and a motherly manner, sat inside, dispensing wondrous lemon, cappuccino, and chocolate ices.

As we headed toward Alvie's enjoying our ices, I said, "That Meredith sure seemed busy. I don't think she'd have the time in her schedule to commit a crime."

"Well, according to her date book, she's scheduled for a lot of parties," Mackenzie said. "But I'll bet she's not too busy to squeeze in a murder or two, if she really wanted to."

There was no point in arguing with her. I knew I was right about Meredith, though. We walked to Alvie's without saying another word.

The Five-Finger Discounter

It was after school Tuesday before we had a chance to stop in at the Central Park precinct. Police stations always have an odor of tobacco, leather, gunpowder, and fear about them. This one was no different.

When we walked into his office, Lieutenant Douglas was just taking a gulp from his massive coffee cup. That explained the circles under his eyes. I wondered how he could ever get to sleep.

We brought him up to date on our firsthand encounters with the ninja stalker James Nichols and the ambitious rainmaker Meredith Claiborne.

"There's one suspect we haven't had a chance to interview yet," I said. "Willy Corbin, the hospital janitor who got canned for stealing."

"We've already paid him a visit," said Lieutenant Douglas.

"What did you find out?" Mackenzie asked.

"One thing's for sure, even if he isn't our phantom, he's guilty of something," Lieutenant Douglas said. "His apartment was a classic thief's den, filled with boxes of stuff—electronics, designer clothing, pharmaceuticals. . . ."

"Let me guess," I said. "You asked him about the stuff, and he gave you a story about a cousin on Long Island in the import-export biz who was using his apartment for temporary storage."

"It was an uncle in Jersey, but yeah, that was the story," said the lieutenant. "The guy's part of a fencing ring, no doubt about it. We're investigating."

"Anything else?" Mackenzie asked.

"Yeah," said Lieutenant Douglas. "I looked into his records. He was evaluated by a court psychiatrist while being held at a juvenile facility, and the shrink found him to be 'antisocial with psychopathic tendencies, unresolved conflicts of an oedipal nature, and anger-management difficulties.' That's a quote. A sicko, in other words."

I nodded. "So it's possible he's our phantom."

"Could be," said the lieutenant. "Only problem is, we've got no evidence."

"Maybe we can help with that," said Mackenzie. We thanked the lieutenant and told him we'd be in touch.

Outside the precinct, Mackenzie turned to me. "So when are we going to visit Corbin?"

"Now." We hailed a cab and gave the driver Corbin's address in Queens. Settling into the backseat, I said, "I've got the feeling that Corbin's our guy."

"I don't know, P.C. Let's wait and see."

* * *

Corbin lived in a rundown neighborhood full of ram-shackle rowhouses in a building that was located not two hundred yards from the end of one of LaGuardia's busiest runways. The earsplitting roar of jets taking off tore the air every six minutes like clockwork.

"No sane person would live in here," I shouted at Mackenzie over the roar of a passing 727.

"If he did, he'd go crazy in a week," she shouted back.

We checked out Corbin's building. A deli delivery guy, who had just locked his bike to a No Standing Zone sign, walked up and rang the intercom. A moment later, Mackenzie skipped up behind him as he was buzzed in, and slipped her foot in the door before it could latch shut. She waited until the delivery guy had disappeared down the corridor, then opened the door wide. "Let's go," she said, beckoning to me.

We were in.

As we walked in, an unsanitary odor of boiled cab-bage, rotting pork, and mildew tripped my gag reflex. "Egads," I said. "Smells like someone died last week and hasn't been found yet."

"*And* left a plate of sauerkraut to rot on the table," Mac added, wrinkling her nose.

Since there was no elevator, we had to walk the nar-row, rickety staircase up to the fourth floor. "Here we are, number forty-three," I said.

"Here goes nothing," Mackenzie said. She rapped hard on the door.

A few seconds later the door opened a crack. A middle-aged guy with long, scraggly hair, a patchy beard, and bad skin squinted out at us. "What?"

"Good day, sir," I said in a tone of imbecilic good cheer. "I was wondering if you'd heard the Good News."

Corbin started to shut the door.

"Did you know that God is watching you this very instant?" Mackenzie said. "And He doesn't like what He sees."

Corbin couldn't resist responding. "Oh yeah? If God don't like what He sees, tell Him to buzz off. And you can buzz off too—"

"It's not that simple," I said. "If we could come in and explain it, you might—"

Corbin slammed the door shut.

Mackenzie and I exchanged a glance, then she rapped on the door again.

He opened it. "Go away."

"Please, sir," said Mackenzie, taking a different tack. "We're on assignment from the church, and we haven't had a convert all day. We really, really need to talk to you."

She sounded so sincere, I almost believed her myself.

Corbin stepped back and ogled Mac, taking in her above-the-knee gold lamé skirt, green army shirt, and blond hair held in place with three strategically placed chopsticks.

"You don't look like a church lady," he said. Then, before she could say anything, he added, "Sure, you can come in—for ten bucks."

I rolled my eyes, but Mackenzie dug in her Campbell's soup can purse and handed him a ten. He opened the door, Mackenzie went in, and I started in after her. Corbin pressed his hand against my chest.

"The ten was for her," he said. "If you want in, it'll cost you twenty."

Seething, I placed a twenty into his sweaty palm.

"Have you given much thought to the afterlife?" Mackenzie asked, and proceeded to berate the poor sap for the next ten minutes. The thirty dollars couldn't have been worth it.

While Mac wrestled Satan for possession of Corbin's eternal soul, I took a look around. Down a dank and darkened hall I could see boxes labeled with names like Sony, IBM, Nintendo, and Hewlett-Packard. TVs, computers, video-game consoles, pagers, cell phones—all of them hot as chili peppers, no doubt.

Through a partially open door I could see into the back room, where Corbin had set up on an old steel desk a computer with an oversize monitor, along with a scanner/fax/printer and an ethernet connection, plus an X-Box, PlayStation 2, and GameCube consoles. The various components were hooked up in a spaghetti platter of wires and cables. There was even what looked like an industrial networking router. For an unemployed criminal janitor who couldn't spell, Corbin appeared to be pretty computer literate.

Meanwhile, Mackenzie was steering the conversation around to more personal topics. "Do you have a job, Willy?" she said in a concerned tone. Apparently she was on a first-name basis with him now.

"Nah, not anymore. I used to work at a hospital."

"You were laid off?" Mackenzie asked.

"Canned," Corbin said, almost proudly. "Some jerk nurse accused me of stealing."

"And did you steal, Willy?" she asked, her eyes practically welling up with concern for his soul. What an actress!

"What if I did?" Corbin shot back. "The cops couldn't prove nothing. Listen, I'm sick of answering your stupid questions. Everyone keeps asking me about that lousy nurse who got killed. The cops came here and grilled me the other day. It ain't my fault she ran in front of a car!"

"You didn't have anything to do with it, Willy?" Mackenzie said.

"She was a nasty witch, but I didn't knock her off," Corbin said. "And I didn't kill Baio, though it don't exactly break my heart that he's dead either."

"Someone's been sending threatening e-mails to the hospital," I said, jumping in.

"I don't know nothing about that," Corbin replied heatedly. "I don't even own a computer."

"Really?" I said. "That's funny, because I noticed through that door—"

"Hey, wait a second. How did you know about the e-mails?" Corbin demanded. He took a step toward me. "You ain't no God squad. You got your thirty bucks' worth of my time. Now get out of here before I throw you out."

I had my doubts about whether Corbin could take both Mackenzie and me at the same time. With his scrawny arms and potbelly, he wasn't exactly the most physically imposing specimen of all time.

I can take care of myself, and Mackenzie knows how to dish it out when she needs to. I've seen her reduce tougher guys than Corbin to watery messes on the floor with one well-aimed kick. But there seemed to be no point in provoking him further. We'd seen what we'd needed to see.

"All right, we're going," I said, and we beat a hasty retreat. As we clattered down the stairs, I asked Mackenzie, "Do you think he did it?"

"Hard to say," she said as we emerged from the building into the relatively fresh air of Queens. "He was weirdly truthful, in his own way. He didn't mind telling us he'd been accused of robbery, and he didn't even deny it was true."

"Confessing to petty theft is different from confessing

to murder, though. One'll bring you a year or two in the pokey. The other might mean you'll be facing a hot squat."

Mackenzie nodded. "I think we may have to pay him a return visit sometime."

6

Déjà Vu All Over Again

That night, Jesus and I had dinner with the Riggses. Dad had been called out of town that morning to help excavate an early African American cemetery in Savannah, Georgia. As promised, Mac's dad, Dr. Riggs, had made moussaka, one of his specialties.

I met Jesus in the lobby of Mac's building. He zipped over to me in his motorized chair, a prize I'd helped him acquire during the solving of a murder at the Natural History Museum. "Whassup, dude?" he said.

We tapped knuckles. "*Nada mucho, amigo,*" I said in intentionally idiotic Spanish. Then I filled him in on Corbin's collection of toys.

"PlayStation, GameCube, *and* X-Box?" said Jesus. "It's a wonder the guy ever leaves his apartment."

"Judging from his pasty complexion, I'd say he doesn't get out much."

"That's bad, man." Jesus shook his head. "I mean, I love my 'puter, but even I know when it's time to get out and get some exercise. Feel this."

He flexed his arm, and I squeezed his biceps. "Not bad."

"Working out. I got a bar set up in the doorway of my room. Forty pull-ups, three times a day. My mom used to complain about whacking her forehead on the bar, but now she ducks without even thinking about it. Which is cool, because when Mom's unhappy, everyone's unhappy."

Over dinner, between bites of succulent eggplant, I quizzed Mackenzie's mom on Rubén Baio's and Amanda Griffith's autopsies.

"Baio died of a puncture wound to the left ventricle of the heart," said Mrs. Riggs said. "The blade was very thin and extremely sharp, almost certainly a surgeon's scalpel. Probably a Swann-Morton E11 or a similar surgical blade."

"What about Amanda?" I asked.

"Death was the result of multiple internal injuries," said Mrs. Riggs. "Trauma to the liver, spleen, and kidneys, as well as severe subdural hematoma. Basically, she bled to death internally."

I swallowed. "What caused the cuts on her neck and back?"

"We're still not certain," she answered. "They appear to have been made by a very sharp serrated blade. Could have been a medical instrument of some kind, such as a sternum saw."

"Or a knife with a serrated edge, like some ninjas used to carry?" I asked.

"Possibly."

I looked at Mackenzie. It looked like James Nichols was shaping up into our number-one suspect. He had motive, opportunity, and his choice of about a zillion sharp-edged weapons.

Mackenzie asked her father about the psychology of the phantom bus murderer.

"My guess is the killer is most likely a person who is entirely used to getting his way," said Dr. Riggs. "The intimacy of the attacks—a scalpel to the heart, slashes to the back of the head—indicate unresolved frustration. That the attacks took place in public show that the murderer at some level wanted the victims—and their friends and loved ones—to know *why* they were being killed."

"You think the motivation was revenge, then?" Mac asked.

"Possibly," her dad said. "Unconsciously the killer *wants* to be caught—a phenomenon not uncommon among serial killers. Look at Son of Sam, back in the 1970s—he sent notes to the police practically begging them to stop him. Often killers are themselves experts on the psychology of killing."

"Like Ted Bundy, who was a fan of Charles Manson," I remarked.

"Funny you should mention those two," said Jesus. "I was digging around the other day into James Nichols's background. In addition to writing a couple of books about ninjas, he's also edited several on serial killers, including Manson and Bundy."

I whistled. "Fits the profile to a T. From what we've seen of the way he treats the people he works with, he's definitely used to getting his way. The martial-arts obsession shows he's got a violent streak. He had to be physically thrown out of the hospital. *And* he's got a thing for serial killers."

"P.C., *you've* got a thing for serial killers," Mackenzie pointed out, "but that doesn't make you a murderer."

"Without jumping to any conclusions," said Dr. Riggs, "I could see how, if Nichols had felt rejected by Amanda Griffith, his stalking might escalate to murder. But why would he kill Rubén Baio first? It doesn't fit."

"Maybe he thought Amanda and Rubén had a thing going," I said. "Eliminate the competition."

"But no one at the hospital—not the head nurse, not Brini Thompson, who claimed to have been Amanda's close friend—mentioned that they were seeing each other," Mackenzie argued.

"Maybe they weren't," I said. "But that doesn't mean Nichols couldn't have got it in his head that they were. We're not dealing with a rational man here."

Mackenzie looked doubtful. "Seems like a stretch, P.C. Let's face it, Nichols had much less of an alibi to kill Rubén Baio than Willy Corbin did. Or Meredith Claiborne, for that matter."

"Meredith didn't kill anybody!" I said, banging my fork down on my plate.

The table fell silent.

"Sorry," I muttered. "It's just that I'm sure she's innocent."

Again no one said anything for a several long seconds. Finally Jesus broke the silence. "I pulled up the hospital's records on Meredith Claiborne's lawsuit." (I noticed Mrs. Riggs roll her eyes at the mention of Jesus's semi-legal snooping.) "Turns out that Meredith was medicating her mother with Demerol, but her HMO had only approved generic drugs, not brand-name ones. It was Meredith's mucking around with the treatments that made her lose her case against the hospital."

"She lost on a technicality?" I said, exasperated. "So what if she was giving her mom extra painkillers? If the doctors had treated her properly, she wouldn't have needed the painkillers in the first place. Maybe she wouldn't have died!"

Another conversation killer.

After a few minutes, Dr. Riggs got the discussion going again. "It's interesting that this killer has become known to the tabloids as the Phantom of Eighty-sixth Street," he said. "It fits in perfectly with my own theory of the psychology of the killer—that of a frustrated control freak unable to restrain his darker impulses. If we don't deal with them, our inner phantoms, the ones that lurk in our unconscious, will come after us and erupt."

"When we least expect it," added Mackenzie.

"Exactly," said her dad. "These phantoms guard the

pain we feel. The pain of loss. Phantom pain itself, from a lost limb, is the physical manifestation of what I believe is essentially a psychological process: the life-long coming to terms we all must make with our own mortality."

Dr. Riggs looked around the table. "We have baklava for dessert. P.C., do you mind helping me serve?"

"Sure, Dr. R."

We were alone in the kitchen, Dr. Riggs busily slicing up the baklava while I assembled forks and plates. "Mackenzie's worried about you, you know," he said.

I didn't say anything.

"She wonders if you've ever dealt effectively with your mother's death," he went on. "I've wondered the same thing."

I sighed. "I keep thinking that if I just don't think about it, maybe I won't feel so bad. It doesn't work, though."

"Hiding from pain never works," he said.

"Lately it's been worse," I admitted. "I don't know why."

"When did it start?" he asked.

I thought about it for a minute. "In the park, the night Mackenzie and I went to see the Philharmonic."

"What was it about that night?"

"I don't know. . . . Yes I do. It was seeing a little kid being hugged by his mom and dad." I turned away so that Dr. Riggs couldn't see my eyes start to well up. "We used to go to the park, Mom and Dad and me."

"You miss her," said Dr. Riggs. "Of course you do. It's only been a year. The pain is intense now, and it seems like it'll never go away. But give it time. In the meanwhile, it's okay to talk about it. Mackenzie cares about you a lot."

"I know she does."

"Our personal demons can sneak up on us from unexpected directions, you know," said Dr. Riggs. "Like what happened in the park. The unconscious mind is a mysterious thing. We'll be looking one way, and our phantoms will pull a surprise attack from another."

We had just loaded the dessert plates onto a tray when we heard cries of distress coming from the other room.

Bursting into the dining room, I asked, "What is it? What's the matter?"

"The Phantom struck again," said Mackenzie. She turned up the volume on the TV.

A reporter was standing against a backdrop of flashing lights. "I'm standing at the corner of Park Avenue and Eighty-sixth Street," she said, "where yet another employee of Presbyterian Hospital has been murdered. The victim's name is Jeannie Close, head nurse of the oncology unit."

Mackenzie gasped. "Oh, no!"

We listened to the rest of the report. There wasn't much more hard information, beyond the victim's name and the fact that she'd been killed while riding the

Eighty-sixth Street crosstown bus. We watched, mesmerized, as the words *The Phantom of Eighty-sixth Street* scrolled by on the bottom of the screen.

"Mackenzie, P.C.," said Mrs. Riggs, "I want you off this case. It's getting too dangerous. Let the police handle it."

"Sorry, Mom, but we can't drop it now," Mackenzie said. "We just spoke to Jeannie Close a few days ago. We're involved now. We have to see it through to the end."

We were out the door before anyone could stop us.

"Be careful, guys!" Jesus called after us.

"Don't worry," I said.

Without either of us even having to say a word, we both knew where we were headed—Eighty-sixth and Park, where we were sure we'd find Lieutenant Douglas working the case.

The crime scene was a circus—ambulances, police cruisers, paddy wagons, fire engines. Four different local TV news trucks, plus three cable outlets. A talk-radio station had set up a table on the sidewalk, and the nighttime shock-jock was taking calls. Scanning the crowd for Lieutenant Douglas, we spotted him talking to a burly guy in a blue Metropolitan Transit Authority jacket—the bus driver. We sidled up to catch the end of their conversation.

"I didn't notice anything," the driver was saying. "It was just another quiet night. Most of my passengers are regulars—the same faces every day. That nurse who got killed, she was one. Been riding my route for years now. A nice lady. I didn't even know her name."

"And you say you didn't see anybody suspicious?" said Lieutenant Douglas.

"No sir."

"Who noticed that she was dead?"

"She was sitting on the right side of the aisle. Sitting real still, her eyes closed, like she was asleep. Lots of passengers fall asleep on the bus after a long day at work. . . ."

"Go on," said the lieutenant.

"So we came to the stop here, and she just sort of falls over, real slow, into the aisle. A lady screamed, and I got out of my seat to see what the matter was. She had a big old needle stuck in her neck."

Lieutenant Douglas nodded. The bus driver went on, describing how several passengers called 911 on their cell phones. The police had arrived within minutes. No one on the bus seemed to be the perpetrator, however. Nurse Close had been sitting motionless—presumably dead—since the bus was halfway across the park. Whoever had killed her was long gone.

When Lieutenant Douglas was done with the bus driver, Mackenzie and I went up to him.

"We couldn't help overhearing your interview with the driver," I said. "Is it true she was found with a needle in her neck?"

Lieutenant Douglas nodded. "Standard disposable

hypodermic. Used by thousands of medical personnel every day, not to mention hundreds of junkies."

"What do you think killed her?" Mac asked.

"Paramedics said it could have been a number of things," said the lieutenant. "One of the pento barbitols is the most likely. It's what vets use to put dogs to sleep. It kills instantly."

A bunch of cops trooped out of the bus, along with crime-scene technicians in white scrubs and several plainclothes officers.

"Do you mind if we take a look inside the bus?" I asked the lieutenant.

After consulting with a couple of the crime-scene guys, he gave us the okay.

A chalk outline had been drawn where Nurse Close had fallen in the aisle. She'd been sitting in one of the forward-facing seats.

"Whoever stuck her with the needle must have been sitting on the bench right behind her," I said.

The bus's rear exit was just across the aisle—convenient for a quick escape after the dirty work was done. Mackenzie was down on her hands and knees, looking under the seat where Nurse Close had been when she was murdered.

"The crime-scene guys already came through here," I said.

"I know. Sometimes people miss things though. Like this."

I went over to her. "What is it?"

"Don't know—it looks like some kind of straw."

She handed it to me. It was a very thin, flexible plastic straw, about six inches long, similar to but narrower than the kind that comes with juice boxes.

"Let's hold on to it. It may be a clue."

Mac slipped it into her faux alligator-skin handbag. "Let's get on home. It's late."

In the taxi on the way back to the West Side, I said, "We should have done something to stop this murder from happening."

"What could we have done, P.C.?"

"I don't know. Warn the hospital staff, maybe?" I stared out the window, adding up what we knew about the case. Then it hit me. "What's today?"

"Wednesday."

"No, I mean the date."

"The eighteenth. Why?"

"There's a pattern, don't you see? The first murder was on the twelfth, the second on the fifteenth. And now tonight, the eighteenth. Every three days the Phantom treats another victim to a dirt nap."

"That means we've only got three days to catch him before he strikes again. . . . But maybe Nurse Close was the last," Mackenzie said, hopefully. "Maybe the Phantom's spree is over."

"I don't think so, Mac. Do you?"

Mackenzie sat quietly for a moment. The taxi passed

through a huge, spooky plume of steam issuing from a grate in the street. "The top of my head is tingling like crazy," she said. "I think you're right. This thing isn't over yet."

That's it. Whenever Mac's head tingles, it means that something's not right.

"This time we're going to stop him," I said.

There was no way we could let another innocent person fall prey to this homicidal maniac.

Shadowing

The moment the bell rang the next day at school, I shoved my chemistry book into my backpack with all the rest of my junk: a Baggie full of emergency gummi worms; sixty cents in loose change; a key-chain flashlight with my house keys. Also a warthog tusk with ancient carvings brought back by my dad from one of his digs; a portable CD player with a Strokes CD inside, along with a Radiohead CD for when I got sick of the Strokes; a Polaroid of my mom and me Rollerblading through Battery Park a couple of years before; and at the very bottom, in the creases, pencil shavings, sand from Jones Beach, and miscellaneous grit.

Then I grabbed Mackenzie. "Let's go, Mac," I said. "We gotta hit Food Emporium."

"Run out of gummi worms already?" she asked.

"As a matter of fact, no," I said. "Care for one?"

She shook her head. "Why the supermarket then?"

"We need to find a match for that straw you found last night. It might tell us something about the killer."

* * *

The manager at Food Emporium held the straw between finger and thumb and peered at it through his trifocals for a few seconds. Then he twitched his cheesy little Rhett Butler mustache and said, "Nope."

"Nope what?" I asked.

"Nope, nothing like that here. It's not from a juice box. It's too thin to be a drinking straw. It's too long to be a cocktail straw." He handed it back to Mackenzie. "Try a hardware store."

"Thanks anyway," Mackenzie said.

On the way to find a hardware store, we stopped to pay a visit on Lieutenant Douglas at the precinct house.

"Do you have anything new?" I asked him.

"Right now we're proceeding on the assumption that it is a serial killer," he said. "One murder is a tragedy. Two is an unlikely coincidence. But when you have three murders, all on the same bus, and the victims all knew each other—that's not a coincidence. That's the work of a serial killer. We have to assume the Phantom will strike again."

"Have you gotten the lab reports back on Nurse Close yet?" Mackenzie asked.

"Your mother's fast, and she does good work. As we suspected, Close was killed with pento barbitol— enough to knock out a rhino. Death would have been instantaneous."

"And no one saw anything?" I asked.

"We interviewed all the passengers we could find,"

said Lieutenant Douglas. "No one saw anything."

"Hmmm . . . sounds like the Phantom operates like a real phantom," I said.

"What about the hypodermic?" Mackenzie asked.

"It was clean. No prints or fibers. Here, take a look at these," he said, handing us a folder full of eight-by-ten glossies.

They were the standard crime-scene snaps. Dead bodies don't look like they do in the movies. There's something undefinably awkward, unnatural—*inhuman*—about a corpse.

"What's that?" I asked pointing to a spot on Nurse Close's neck.

"That's the puncture wound from the needle," said the lieutenant.

"No, I mean surrounding it. There's a red area about the size of a quarter surrounding the puncture."

"We're not sure what that is," he said. "It may be just an unusual surface reaction to the pento barbitol. Looks like some kind of burn, though. They're still running tests."

"Have you asked Willy Corbin and Jim Nichols where they were last night at the time of the murders?" I asked.

"Nichols claims he was out shopping, and Corbin says he was at home watching a *Law and Order* marathon," said the lieutenant. "No alibis for either one."

"What about Meredith Claiborne?" Mackenzie asked.

"We've spoken to her," said Lieutenant Douglas. "She was out drinking with some coworkers last night."

"So she had an alibi," I said.

"Not an airtight one. She left the bar before the murder occurred. But the concierge at her building said she practically fell out of the cab, she was so drunk."

"Doesn't sound like she could have murdered anyone last night," I said.

"P.C.—" Mackenzie started to say.

I interrupted her. "I say Nichols, with his history of stalking, and his obsession with martial arts and serial killers, is still our prime suspect."

Mackenzie didn't answer. She just looked at me.

After an uncomfortable silence, Lieutenant Douglas said, "Claiborne's secretary has provided alibis for her whereabouts during all three murders. We haven't ruled her out completely as a suspect, but I'm inclined to agree that it's Nichols."

It was almost five o'clock by the time we left the police station. Mackenzie and I decided to walk over to the Bransford & Hill building and stake out Nichols. At twenty after, Nichols came out, gym bag in hand.

"Let's go," I whispered to Mackenzie as Nichols crossed Fifth Avenue and headed west on Fifty-second Street. Making sure to keep a hundred yards behind him, but never letting him leave our sight, we trailed him to a health club on Ninth Avenue.

Stonecypher's was one of those gyms where the front is all glass, so that the people inside pumping iron, or rowing, or hamstering on treadmills, can be seen by every passerby on the sidewalk. Mackenzie and I waited outside while Nichols chatted with the guy behind the counter, then disappeared through a door in the back.

Judging from the bulging veins, oversized jaws, and prominent brow ridges on display, I wondered if the gym was a "juice bar"—a gym where illegal steroids were for sale.

"Be right back," I said to Mackenzie, and started through the door.

Going up to the Neanderthal behind the counter, I said, "I'm thinking about joining a gym to bulk up. How long would it take me to get as big as that guy who just came in?"

"You?" he said, looking me up and down and poking my upper arm. "A pipsqueak like you could never get that big. At least not without some serious help."

"You mean a personal trainer?"

"Personal trainer, hah!" he laughed. "You need a personal pharmacist. Nobody looks like that guy without chemical assistance."

"That's all I wanted to know." I thanked him and went back outside.

"What did you find out?" Mackenzie asked.

"Why Nichols gets testy so easily," I said. "He uses

steroids the way an albino uses sunblock. That stuff'll rot your brain, to say nothing of what it does to your kidneys and liver. He's a walking time bomb, if you ask me."

Deadline

In light of the approaching murder deadline, Mackenzie and I decided to split up the sleuthing chores the next day. "I'll take Meredith, if you take the hardware store," I said over the phone.

"You're sure you're up for it?"

"Don't worry. I don't think she's our perp, but I can put my personal prejudices aside. I'll investigate her the way I would any other suspect."

"Okay. And I'll see what I can find out about our mystery straw."

Meredith Claiborne lived in a high-rise on the Upper East Side, near Rockefeller University. I was just entering the lobby of her building when she and a middle-aged woman in a dark-green jacket came out of the elevator. I ducked out of sight behind a large concrete planter. Peeking through ficus leaves, I eavesdropped on their conversation.

"We'll need to get your apartment repainted before we can show it," said the woman in red. I saw that she was holding a bag that had PRIMETIME REALTY printed on it.

"Call my secretary," Meredith said, racing out of the lobby, toting a bulging shoulder bag and a briefcase.

"But—" was all the realtor lady got out before Meredith had booked it out the door. I wondered how many minutes Meredith had given her before her time had run out. She was turning to go back to the elevator when I emerged from behind the foliage.

"Excuse me," I said. "I'm looking for an apartment for me and my mother. Do you know who I could talk to to find out if this building has any vacancies?"

"You're in luck!" said the woman. She held out her hand. "Vicki Milnik, PrimeTime Realty platinum-level agent. I manage this building."

"What a coincidence!" I exclaimed. I wove a convincing story about how Mom (a podiatrist) and I wanted to move closer to her work and my school (Dalton).

"There's a two-bedroom on the eighth floor that sounds perfect for you and your mother, P.C.," Vicki said. "I'm really not supposed to show it till next week, but I'll bend the rules for you."

"Gosh, thanks," I said.

We went up to eighth floor, where she showed me an apartment that was twice as big as mine. "Um . . . it's nice," I said. "But we're looking for something a little bigger. That lady you were talking to when I first came into the lobby—"

"Ms. Claiborne," said Vicki.

"Yeah. Did I hear her say her apartment was coming on the market?"

"That's right."

"Could I see her apartment?"

"I'm afraid not," Vicki said. "I have permission to show it, but it's not ready yet."

"Right," I said, disappointed. That would have been too easy. "Thanks for showing me around, Ms. Milnik."

She handed me her card. "Have your mother call me for an appointment. My office is on the second floor."

"Will do."

We rode the elevator down together to the second floor, where Vicki got off.

"Good luck finding a place, P.C.," she said as the doors closed.

I went down to the lobby, but I didn't leave the building. The apartment I'd seen had a back door that led to the emergency stairwell and service elevator. If there's one thing that a detective learns, it's that what looks like trash to the untrained eye may contain valuable clues. Maybe I'd find something in Meredith's garbage— something that proved she couldn't be the murderer, something that would put Mackenzie's suspicions to rest.

I followed a narrow, zigzag corridor that shot off the back of the lobby and took the service elevator up to Meredith's apartment on the thirty-seventh floor. The first thing I noticed in the service area behind

79

Meredith's apartment was the smell of liquor. Her blue recycling bin was filled to the brim with empty tequila, gin, and vodka bottles. Next to the recycling bin was a twenty-gallon black garbage bag. Carefully I untwisted the tie. Apple peelings, the Styrofoam takeout containers, junk mail, used Kleenex, a pair of worn-out shoes. Nothing out of the ordinary.

I was about to give up when a couple of crumpled up receipts caught my eye. I slipped them into my pocket and left to meet Mackenzie at the Roosevelt Island tramway entrance. At least I'd have something to show for my investigation. Mac couldn't accuse me of shirking, just because I was convinced Nichols was the culprit.

"So what did you find out about the straw?" I asked Mackenzie when we met up.

"I took the mystery straw to Murray's Hardware on Sutton Place. It's similar to the straws that come with cans of aerosol lubricant, but it's not an exact match. I showed it to Murray himself. He said he couldn't recall seeing anything quite like it."

"We'll keep working on it," I said.

Just then my cell phone chirped. It was Jesus.

"Whatcha got?" I asked him.

"Dude, I was finally able to trace those threatening e-mails the hospital's been getting."

"And?"

"They came from a Hotmail account registered to one William L. Corbin."

"Bingo," I said. "Thanks, Jesus."

I hung up. "Next stop: a return visit to Willy Corbin's."

Corbin greeted us with his usual charm. "What the hell do you freaks want?"

He looked, and smelled, like he hadn't bathed since the last time we'd seen him. His hair was a rat's nest of tangles, and he was wearing the same sweat-stained JUDAS PRIEST *METAL MELTDOWN* 1998 WORLD TOUR T-shirt he'd been wearing when we'd seen him the first time.

I waited for a jet to clear the airspace above our heads to respond. I'd had enough pussyfooting around. It was time to confront him with our suspicions. Go for the jugular.

"We know you've been sending threatening e-mails to the hospital you used to work at," I said.

"I don't know what you're talking about." His breath smelled like rancid cottage cheese.

"A friend of ours traced them back to your Hotmail account. You're a talented hacker, Corbin, but you're no match for our friend."

"Take a hike," he shot back. "Before I throw you both down the stairs."

"We could have the police search your computer," I said. "Even if you erased the messages, there'll still be a record of them in your hard drive."

Corbin grew red in the face. He looked like he was about to leap forward and wring my neck. "I'll kill you!" he shouted.

"Just like you killed Rubén Baio and Amanda Griffith?" I shot back. "Is that how you take care of everyone who crosses you? By murdering them?"

"You're crazy!" he screamed. "I didn't kill anybody! And you can't prove I sent those e-mails. Now get out before I wring your neck!" He retreated into his apartment, slamming the door behind him so hard that something inside crashed to the floor.

A jet rumbled by overhead.

"Nice work," Mackenzie said as we made our way down the stairwell. "If Corbin really is the maniac, you sure put him in a good mood."

It was getting to be almost dinnertime. Back in the city, we decided to grab a quick bite at the Cosmic Café. Over burgers, we did our addition on the case.

"Wait a second," I said. "I just remembered something." I dug into my pants pocket and drew out a couple of wrinkled strips of paper. "Receipts. I got them out of Meredith's trash."

I smoothed them on the table. One was from the Empire Bookstore—Meredith had bought a couple of mysteries, a vacation guide to Mexico, and a tax-tips guide.

"Nothing too incriminating there," I said.

"What about the other one?"

The second receipt was from East End Drugs—cold medicine, a toothbrush, some soap. Something called fz spray.

"What's fz spray?" Mackenzie asked.

I frowned. "No idea. I'm sure it's nothing important."

"I think we should check it out, P.C."

I grunted, and took a bite of my burger.

After dessert, we paid the tab and hit the sidewalk again. Just across the street from the Cosmic Cafe was a drugstore. I showed the receipt to the pharmacist on duty.

"This isn't from this store," he pointed out.

"I know. I'm not looking for a refund. I just want to know what one of the items is—fz spray. Would you have any ideas about what that would be?"

With his middle finger the pharmacist shoved his glasses back up to the top of his nose. "Stands for 'freeze spray.' Diabetics use it to make injections painless. A squirt of the stuff freezes the skin so you can't feel anything. Aisle four."

We went to aisle four and checked out the freeze-spray cans on the shelf. The cans came with little straws taped to their sides.

"Perfect match," said Mackenzie, holding up the straw she'd found on the bus against one of the cans.

"That still doesn't make Meredith the Phantom," I said. "She probably had to give her mother plenty of shots. Anyone could have bought one of these freeze sprays. It's hardly a smoking gun."

Mackenzie gave me a long look. "Whatever," she said at last, and put the straw back in her handbag.

9

Lean, Mean Killing Machine

I glanced at my watch. Quarter after seven. "It's still early. Let's run over to Presbyterian and do a little snooping around—see if we can figure out who's next on the killer's list."

"All right," said Mac.

We took the subway. By the time we emerged from the 103rd Street stop, the sun had sunk below the massive prewar apartment buildings that line West End Avenue. The streets were almost empty, and a hard wind off the Hudson chilled the evening air. A lone seagull perched on a streetlamp and squawked raucously at us as we passed.

Visiting hours were over at seven, so we couldn't just waltz through the main lobby, as we had the first time. A stone-faced guard looked suspiciously at us as we loitered near the information desk.

"What do we do?" Mackenzie whispered, trying to look inconspicuous. "Come back tomorrow?"

"No. There's got to be another way up besides the main elevators." I remembered how I'd gotten to

Meredith Claiborne's back door earlier in the day. "Let's find the service elevator."

"Good idea."

When the security guard's back was turned, we slipped through a door marked HOSPITAL PERSONNEL ONLY. Behind the door was a web of cubicles, administrative offices, and conference rooms. A bunch of pencil pushers were still at their desks, so Mackenzie and I tried to walk by them in such a way that it looked as if we knew where we were going. It would have been nice if we had, or if there had been signs pointing to an exit, but we didn't and there weren't, so we just plunged deeper into the network of hallways.

"Look," Mackenzie said, nudging me. "A stairwell."

We made a beeline for it, but unfortunately it went only down, into the basement, not up to the rest of the hospital.

"Let's give it a shot," I said. "Maybe we can find the service elevator from the basement."

We walked down a flight, but the door to the basement was shut and locked from the other side. Same with the subbasement.

"One more?" I asked.

"What have we got to lose?"

Fortunately, the door to the subsubbasement was open. Unfortunately, the subsubbasement seemed to be where the staff stored all the junk and refuse that didn't belong anywhere else in the hospital. We groped our way down the creepy hallway. Suddenly a loud *bang* sounded not five feet from where we were standing.

"What was that?" Mackenzie whispered.

"Just a heating pipe expanding," I said. It was all I could do to keep my own voice from cracking.

After I don't know how long—ten, fifteen minutes—of nerve-racking wandering through the subsubbasement, we found an elevator and rode it back up to the ground floor. Just as the doors slid open, I was saying, "Okay, now let's see if we can—"

"Aaagh!" Mackenzie and I screamed at the same time. We'd stepped off the elevator smack into a corpse. It was lying on a gurney, covered in a white sheet except for a small bit of bluish-gray toe.

We carefully stepped around the gurney.

"All we have to do is get to the fifth floor, poke around, and get out of here," I said, trying to act brave. "Look, a staircase. We're golden."

Just before we got there, I grabbed Mac's arm. "Shhh!"

We froze.

"What?" she whispered.

"I thought I heard something," I whispered back. "In the stairwell. Behind us. Footsteps."

Neither of us made a sound. It was so quiet I could swear I heard my heart thumping in my chest.

After a minute, Mackenzie finally said, "You must've been hearing the echoes of our footsteps."

I nodded. "I guess you're right. Come on, we made it."

We'd come out into an area of the fifth floor that we didn't see on our earlier visit. It looked like there was a renovation going on. The hall was lined with scaffolding, propane tanks, thirty-gallon buckets for mixing plaster. An enormous scissors lift entirely blocked one corridor, forcing us to follow another, underneath an illuminated arrow and sign that read RADIOLOGY.

"Follow the arrow," Mackenzie said.

"Let's not go that way," I said. I took the key chain flashlight out of my backpack and shone it down the other hall, in the direction of the scissors lift. "We can go that way, if we climb over that thing."

Mackenzie seemed to sense my desperate need not to follow that particular sign. "Sure, P.C. No problem."

We clambered over the scissors lift and ventured down the hallway. The floor had been ripped clean of its linoleum, so we were walking on the bare concrete. The Sheetrock had been removed from the walls, and the insulation was now held in place by huge sheets of billowy plastic stapled to the studs.

"Wait!" Mackenzie whispered, grabbing *my* arm this time. "I heard it. Someone behind us."

"Hello?" I called back toward the scissors lift. No answer. Then—*scrrraaaape!* The sound of someone dragging a metal object over the concrete floor.

"I think we should get out of here, P.C.," Mackenzie said.

"Right behind you," I said.

We grabbed hands and took off blindly down the hallway. In moments we hit a T intersection.

"Left or right?" I panted.

"Eeny, meeny, *left!*" Mackenzie said.

We shot off down the left-hand corridor, which was even darker than the one we'd left behind. My flashlight was totally useless as we charged headlong into blackness. Behind us we could still hear scraping sounds, and the occasional metallic *clank* and *thud*.

"Let's find a door out of here, and quick!" Mackenzie said.

Again we had a choice of left and right. This time I chose right. No idea why. I hadn't the foggiest clue as to how to get out of there.

"Another staircase!" Mackenzie shouted, pointing down yet another hallway.

We slammed hard against the door to the staircase, but it didn't budge—locked from the other side. The scraping sound, the echoing footsteps, were coming closer.

We doubled back a short way, then went down a new hallway—or at least what we thought was a new hallway. We were so discombobulated, we weren't sure whether we'd been there before or not.

This hallway had multiple doors leading off it. We tried them one by one—all locked. It was like we were the "slow" group in a rats-in-a-maze intelligence experiment. We just couldn't figure out how the heck to get out of there. And still the footsteps grew closer.

Finally Mackenzie tried a door that opened, and we ducked inside. We were in a room that was nearly pitch-black. When we tried to lock the door, we discovered we couldn't.

"Great," I groaned. "Now we're trapped."

We leaned against the door, our ears to the cold, smooth metal. We heard the footsteps in the hallway right outside, and then . . .

POW! An explosion detonated inside my head, and I staggered away from the door. Mackenzie did likewise, a look of utter shock and horror on her face. I realized that someone had taken a mighty whack at the door with what sounded like an aluminum baseball bat.

I looked at Mac and she looked at me. Our gaze darted to the doorknob as it started to turn with a slow creaking sound. I grabbed it and turned it back as hard as I could. Whoever was on the other side started pounding on it furiously, like a rabid animal. The pounding went on and on.

Then quiet, followed by a small click. Then nothing.

"What's going on?" Mackenzie asked.

"Dunno," I said, still gripping the doorknob.

Something started to hum—an electrical sort of buzz—at first quietly. It started getting louder. Much louder.

Mackenzie covered her ears. "What the—?"

A red warning light came on above us. In the crimson glow I could make out the sign underneath it: RADIA-TION, along with the triangular nuclear symbol and, very large, very prominent, in English followed by its equivalent in Spanish, French, German, Russian, and what I took to be Arabic, Hebrew, and Chinese: the word *DANGER*.

By the lurid red of the warning light, I could now make out what was in the room with us. It was a sleek bed fit into a sort of giant high-tech C-clamp. I recognized it from my mom's illness as a linear accelerator—a machine that produced the high-energy radiation that could burn away fatal tumors.

The downside was that the radiation itself was highly lethal.

I felt a sinking feeling in the pit of my stomach. Memories of my mom, wasting away, losing her hair, came over me.

"P.C., look!" Mackenzie shouted above the buzzing. She pointed at a gauge set into the wall behind me. The gauge measured radiation, and its needle was moving, now in the yellow, climbing inexorably toward the red.

I whipped out my cell phone but got nothing but static. "The radiation's interfering with the signal!" I shouted.

"Help!" Mackenzie screamed, but there was no way her cries would be heard. The walls of the room would be made of lead, to shield the outside from radiation.

I tried opening the door, but no luck—it was now locked from the outside. The humming was getting louder. I surveyed the room. There was a viewing window in one wall, but no other door. We were trapped. The gauge's needle edged toward the red zone.

"Come here," I yelled, pulling Mackenzie into the corner farthest from the machine. It might not make much of a difference, but if we had to be exposed to deadly radiation, best to minimize the amount. It was all we could do.

We crouched down against the wall in the corner. I felt something grinding into my spine, and turned to look. It was the hinge of a glass door. Inside, set into the wall, was a fire extinguisher.

"Stand back, Mac!" I said, yanking open the door and taking out the fire extinguisher.

"What are you going to do with that?" Mackenzie yelled. "There's no fire in here!"

"The machine produces radiation through magnetism," I shouted. "Watch!"

With all my might I slung the fire extinguisher at the linear accelerator. About halfway to the machine, it got caught in the accelerator's magnetic field and shot like a bullet toward it—right over the bed, underneath the C-clamp overhang—and through to the other side. The fire extinguisher was slung out the far end like a missile and went crashing through the viewing window in a gigantic explosion.

10

Transfer Outta Here

Sensors in the room picked up the breach and immediately shut down the linear accelerator. The buzzing stopped, and the needle on the gauge next to us started easing back down.

Mackenzie and I raced to the shattered window and caught a fleeting glimpse of a hooded figure fleeing through the door of the viewing room.

I helped Mackenzie through the window and then climbed through myself, taking care not to cut myself on the shards of glass still set in the frame.

"Let's catch that freak," I said.

But just as we were leaving the viewing room, three security guards, waving flashlights and nightsticks, arrived at the door. With them was a young doctor in scrubs.

"What in the name of God is going on here?" he demanded. "What are you kids doing?"

"Working on our tans?" Mackenzie offered.

Within minutes the fifth floor was swarming with guards, police, doctors, nurses, technicians, maintenance workers. We told our story to the cops, who obviously weren't buying it—they thought we were just a couple of idiotic vandals—until Lieutenant Douglas arrived and vouched for us.

"They've been working with me," he told the beat cops who'd been giving us a hard time.

The radiologist on duty checked the readings on the gauge, and assured us that we were okay. "Though I'd suggest you don't have any more X rays for a year or two, unless it's an emergency," he added.

Lieutenant Douglas took us downstairs to the hospital cafeteria, where over lukewarm weak coffee and stale Danishes he gave us a lecture.

"I bailed you out upstairs," he said. "But I want you off this case now. It's too dangerous."

"We've only got two more days before the killer strikes again," I said.

"You've got no proof of that," said the lieutenant. "We don't know why the killer has targeted hospital workers. We don't know who the next victim will be. We don't even know if there's going to be a next victim. It might all be over with."

"Corbin must be the killer," I insisted. "He worked here. He could've learned how to work that machine."

"You've got no proof, P.C.," said Lieutenant Douglas. "There are hundreds of hospital employees who could work that machine. To say nothing of the patients."

"But—"

"You're off the case. And that's final."

The next afternoon, as soon as school let out, we raced over to Bransford & Hill Publishers. If we could rule out James Nichols, that left Corbin. We could get Lieutenant Douglas to stake out his apartment and make sure he didn't kill again.

"We've got an eleven o'clock with Jim Nichols," I said to the receptionist in the lobby downstairs.

She picked up the phone. "Whom shall I say is—?"

"Oh, don't bother." I pressed the elevator button, and the doors swooshed open. "He's expecting us."

Inside the elevator, I said to Mackenzie, "I hope she didn't call Nichols anyway. I'd rather have some time to poke around without him knowing we were here."

"I hope this pans out," she said. "We're running out of time."

The elevator doors opened, and we found ourselves face-to-face with Jonathan Mathers, Jim Nichols's assistant.

"I got a call from downstairs, saying a couple of kids were on the way up," he said. "Now, tell me, what's your game?"

"What do you mean?" I asked.

"Come here," he said, and he led us into an empty conference room off the lobby.

He closed the door and turned to us. "I know you're not Livingston Wendsworth's niece and nephew."

"Oh?" said Mackenzie, trying to gut it out. "How would you know that?"

"Livingston's *my* third cousin twice removed. How do you think I got this job? The first time you came by here, I wasn't sure whether you were for real. So I called my dad and asked if Livingston had any nieces or nephews. Turns out he was an only child."

Mackenzie and I didn't say anything. What could we say? The jig was up.

"So who are you?" he demanded.

"We're investigating a murder," I said, leveling with him. "Jim Nichols is one of the suspects."

Jonathan's eyes popped out in surprise. "Murder suspect? You're kidding!"

"You haven't told Nichols we were imposters, have you?"

"I don't tell him anything I don't absolutely have to. I can't stand the jerk. But still, suspected of murder?" He shook his head.

"Maybe you can help us," Mackenzie said. "Have you noticed anything strange about Nichols lately?"

"Strange?" He laughed. "I don't even know where to begin. I mean, he's totally obsessed with ninjas, war books, fighting, torture."

"And you don't feel these are just intellectual pursuits?" I asked.

"Anything else?" Mackenzie asked. "Has he shown any violent tendencies in real life?"

"Oh, man, has he ever," said Jonathan. He was obviously loving this chance to dish about his boss. "At the last Christmas party, Jim and one of the guys in accounting got into a shouting match over a new assistant."

"Great," Mackenzie said, rolling her eyes.

"They wound up wrestling around on the floor. Knocked over a table filled with appetizers. Jim kicked the guy so hard, he broke one of his ribs."

"Not true," came a voice from the doorway.

We all spun around. It was James Nichols.

"It was two ribs, not one," he said. "I didn't know we'd be having a little storytelling session going on."

"Um, you'll excuse me now," Jonathan muttered to Mac and me. He scurried out of the room. I wondered if his third-cousin-twice-removed's influence in the company would be enough to protect him.

"You want to tell me what you two are doing nosing around here?" Nichols said. He looked as if he was about to explode in a burst of steroid-fueled fury. I didn't want to be around when that happened.

"Not particularly," I said.

"Then you better get out."

We dashed to the elevator bank and slapped the down button.

As the doors to the elevator closed between us and Nichols, he yelled, "If I catch either one of you around here again, I'll break more than just a couple of ribs!"

Party Time

"We were lucky to get out of there alive," Mackenzie said. "That freak is two sandwiches short of a picnic."

"Yeah," I said. "But Lieutenant Douglas was right. There's no real proof that he's the killer. Something's missing—something I can't put my finger on."

We were walking up Fifth Avenue. The sidewalk was swarming with office workers who were leaving work early for the weekend.

"We're running out of time, P.C."

"I know. Let's go over the facts again."

"We know Rubén Baio was stabbed in the heart with a scalpel," Mackenzie said, ticking off her fingers. "Amanda Griffith was slashed in the back with some kind of serrated blade, probably a medical saw."

"Jeannie Close was numbed with freeze spray and then given a fatal injection of pento barbitol," I said. "The victims all worked at Presbyterian Hospital. Willy Corbin, Jim Nichols, and Meredith Claiborne all had grievances against the hospital."

"One of them has got to be the killer."

"Corbin and Nichols are the most likely suspects," I insisted. "And we know the killer strikes every three days. We're due for a murder tomorrow night."

We walked in silence, each of us lost in our own thoughts, past FAO Schwarz. Horribly cheerful canned music, meant to put shoppers in a toy-buying mood, assaulted my ears. "Happy, happy," I said. "Let's party!"

Mackenzie stopped. "Yes," she said slowly. "Let's. And I know just the party we should go to."

"What are you talking about? Now's not the time to go to a party! We have a killer to stop!"

"But this is Meredith Claiborne's party," Mackenzie said. "She mentioned it at her office, remember? And I saw it penciled in on her planner. It's at her place, tonight at nine."

"I thought we'd eliminated Meredith as a suspect."

"The fact that she'd bought freeze spray puts her back at the top of my list," Mackenzie argued. "And I've got a lot of other things I'd like to ask her about."

"I think it's a waste of time."

"Humor me," she said.

I didn't like to give in, but she was adamant.

Several hours later we stepped out of a cab in front of Meredith's high-rise. "Keep the change," I told the cabbie, and he pulled away from the curb.

We were dressed to impress in order to fit in with the Upper East Side party crowd. Mackenzie had her hair up in a fancy bun and was wearing a strapless burgundy dress. Her only concession to normal Mac-style was the trusty Doc Martens on her feet. I had on a jacket and tie. Disguised as junior socialites, we scooted past the concierge, rode up to the thirty-seventh floor, and waltzed into Meredith's apartment unchallenged.

"Amazing how people don't question you if you're wearing a coat and tie," I murmured to Mackenzie as we melted into the crowded living room.

"The clothes make the man," she said.

"Make him invisible, in this case."

I scanned the room. "There's Meredith, out on the balcony."

"Let's split up," said Mackenzie. "I'll check out the bathroom—see if she's got any more freeze-sprays lying around. Maybe she has a legitimate use for the stuff."

"I'll check out the bedroom," I said.

"Meet you at the front door in fifteen minutes." She snagged a grilled shrimp from a passing platter and disappeared into the mob.

Trying to act casual, I moved around the edge of the living room toward the hallway that led to the bedroom. Having seen the other apartment in the building, I already knew the layout of Meredith's place. The door to her bedroom was closed, but not locked. Glancing around to make sure nobody was watching me, I quickly turned the knob and slipped inside. In case anyone walked in on me, I took off my jacket—I'd say I was in the bedroom looking for a place to throw my coat.

A queen-size bed, a long, low dresser, a nightstand, an easy chair with reading lamp. Bookcase filled mostly with finance guides and mysteries; several titles like *Beat Cancer Through Meditation!* on alternative medicine. A framed photo on the wall of Meredith and her mother—the same one she had in her office. Nothing suspicious.

I was about to leave when my eye fell on a stack of Polaroids on the dresser. I flipped through them— Meredith with the concierge downstairs, mugging for the camera, making kissy faces. She'd clearly had too much to drink. I flipped the photos over. The time stamp on the back read April 18. The night Jeannie Close was murdered.

Suddenly I heard the doorknob turn behind me. I stuffed the pictures into my pants pocket and spun around, trying to look innocent.

Standing in the doorway was Meredith.

The Ticking Clock

"Get out of my bedroom, you pervert!" she shrieked.

"Okay, okay—"

"What are you, some kind of weirdo stalker?" she spit out.

"He's not a pervert or a stalker, Ms. Claiborne," said Mackenzie from behind her in the hallway.

Meredith wheeled around. "You too? Get out of my apartment, both of you!"

"We're leaving," Mackenzie said. "But you should know we've been investigating the murders of Rubén Baio, Amanda Griffith, and Jeannie Close."

That cooled Meredith right down—froze her, in fact. "I don't know what you're talking about," she croaked.

"Maybe not," Mackenzie said. "But someone tried to boil us in a giant microwave the other night, so this whole thing is getting personal."

"I still don't know—" Meredith started, when she was interrupted by the opening notes of the *William Tell* Overture sounding from the beeper on her nightstand.

Flustered, she crossed the room, picked up the beeper, and turned it off. "Just get out!" she said to us. "Get out now!"

"Not so fast," Mackenzie said, pressing on. "Tell us where you were two nights ago, when Jeannie Close was killed."

"She was here," I said, taking the Polaroids out of my pocket and handing them to Mackenzie. "Take a look. These were taken the night of the murder. She was in no condition to kill anybody."

Mackenzie glanced at them, then placed them on the dresser.

"The police have already questioned me regarding my whereabouts," Meredith said coldly. "I had gone out to a bar with some colleagues after work. I had a little to drink, and came home around seven-thirty. The concierge downstairs saw me. The pictures prove that."

"She's right," I said to Mackenzie.

"I see no reason to answer any further questions. *Now get out of here or I'll press charges!*"

Outside the air was cool and dry. A perfect spring evening. But as we walked downtown to catch the subway home, I was more depressed than ever. "I don't know if we'll ever crack this case," I said to Mackenzie.

"We can't give up now, P.C. We've got less than twenty-four hours to stop another murder."

"I know," I said. I reached into my pocket to get out my MetroCard—only to realize that I still had one of Meredith's Polaroids.

I took it out and showed it to Mac. "Look, I accidentally kept this one."

"Accidentally, maybe. I think my dad would say it was your unconscious at work. What made you hold on to it, P.C.?"

I gazed at the photo. It showed Meredith, arm around the concierge. Red eyes, goofy grin, pale as a sheet. She looked embarrassingly drunk.

"Maybe my subconscious did tell me to keep it," I said. "But I don't know why."

"Sleep on it," Mackenzie said. "Maybe you'll figure it out tomorrow."

I spent most of the next day, Saturday, mulling over the case. It was driving me crazy—the solution was right in front of me, but I couldn't find the key.

Finally, around three in the afternoon, Mackenzie called me up.

"Sleep do you any good?" she asked.

"Nah. Still can't crack it."

"Me neither. I'm so wound up, I haven't been able to eat all day. I need a bagel. Meet me at Starbucks, okay?"

"See you there."

Ten minutes later we were huddled over a table of nosh and java.

"What bothers me most," I said, "is that I feel like we're on the verge of putting the whole thing together." I swallowed a mouthful of lox. "It's like we've got all the pieces of a jigsaw puzzle, but we just can't make them fit. I don't know what to do."

"We could ride the bus back and forth all day, waiting for the murderer to show up," Mackenzie joked, licking a dab of chive cream cheese off her finger. "Just kidding."

"Actually, that's not a bad idea," I said.

As we walked out of Starbucks, Mackenzie said, "You know, I think your depression is catching—now *I* feel it."

"Really?"

"Yeah. I mean, in the last few days we've had each one of our suspects scream at us and threaten us—first Corbin, then Nichols, and then last night, Meredith Claiborne. There's only so much abuse I can take before it begins to get to me," Mackenzie said. "I mean, I keep picturing them, screaming, yelling, the way they went red in the face. . . ."

I went cold all over. "What did you say?"

"I was just saying how getting screamed at gets to me—"

"No, no, after that—about them going red in the face."

I took out the Polaroid of Meredith looking drunk with the concierge.

"What? What is it, P.C.?"

I grabbed her hand and started dragging her uptown, toward the precinct station.

"I know who the Phantom is! I'll explain on the way to the precinct."

"We're here to see Lieutenant Douglas," I told the sergeant on duty at the precinct twenty minutes later.

"Sorry, it's his day off."

"Who's in charge here now?" Mackenzie asked.

"Lieutenant McPhee," said the sergeant. "You got business with him?"

"Yes. Tell him we need to talk to him about the Phantom killer."

The sergeant got up from his desk and disappeared into the back of the station. A few minutes later he reappeared with Lieutenant McPhee.

"What can I do for you?" McPhee asked, settling his large frame into a chair next to the sergeant's.

"Can you reach Lieutenant Douglas for us?" I asked. "We've been working on the Phantom killer case, and—"

"Can't do that," Lieutenant McPhee said. "Man's got to have some time off. Why don't you tell me what the problem is?"

"There's going to be a murder tonight if we don't do anything to stop it," I said.

McPhee settled deeper into his chair. "Okay, start from the beginning."

I took a deep breath. "First off—Meredith Claiborne is the Phantom of the Eighty-sixth Street crosstown bus."

The lieutenant raised his eyebrows. "How do you know?"

"I'll get to that. But first, Meredith's motive: revenge. She blamed the hospital staff on the fifth floor for the death of her mother. Meredith was convinced the doctors and nurses had let her mother suffer needlessly. When she sued the hospital, she lost on a technicality. Meredith is a high-powered financial exec who's used to getting her way. She couldn't deal with that kind of frustration. Seeing her mother mistreated by the hospital, and being unable to find justice in the courts—well, she snapped. Went crazy. Decided to take justice into her own hands."

"A sick kind of poetic justice," Mackenzie added. "Killing hospital staff with medical instruments—a scalpel, a saw, a hypodermic needle."

"Fair enough," said the lieutenant. He had begun to take notes on what we were saying. "You've got motive. And the m.o. fits. What about opportunity?"

"Meredith had plenty of opportunity for the first two murders," I said. "She basically had no alibi. But by the third murder, she knew she was a suspect. Lieutenant Douglas had paid her a visit. So she had to set up an alibi."

"And how'd she do that?" Lieutenant McPhee asked skeptically.

"She went to a bar with some friends after work, and made a big show of getting drunk," Mackenzie said. "When she got home, she made sure the concierge in the lobby knew she was drunk too. You'll find all this in her file."

We waited while he flipped through the file. After a few minutes he looked up and said, "Okay, it's all here—Claiborne's alibi for the night of Close's murder. She was so drunk she could hardly stand up. The concierge confirmed she was crocked. What's the problem?"

"The problem is Meredith *hadn't actually had a drop to drink*. She was faking it. She was actually stone-cold sober."

Lieutenant McPhee gave me a how-the-heck-would-you-know-that look.

"She only *pretended* to be drinking at the bar after work," Mackenzie said. "She wanted to have witnesses vouch that she was so drunk, she couldn't have committed a murder. Just to make sure, she had pictures taken of her flouncing around drunkenly with the concierge."

I took the Polaroid out of my pocket and showed it to the lieutenant.

"Looks pretty out of it to me," he said.

"Looks that way, but isn't," I said. "Here's the thing. The first time we met Meredith, her office was holding a going-away party for one her coworkers and she was drinking champagne. Not nearly as much as she was supposed to have drunk the night Close was killed. And she was as red as a tomato. Mac even asked her about her sunburn."

"That's right," Mackenzie said. "She said that she was allergic to alcohol."

"Take a look at the photo," I said.

"She doesn't look red," Lieutenant McPhee said. "In fact she looks kinda washed out."

"There's no way she'd been drinking that night," I said. "It was a ruse."

"And P.C. found the receipt for the freeze spray that was used to numb Nurse Close's neck for the injection," Mackenzie said. She pulled the receipt from her purse and handed it to Lieutenant McPhee. "It came from Meredith's garbage."

He read it, nodding.

"Every three days she takes out another victim," I said. "She's due again tonight. You've got to arrest her before she kills again."

Lieutenant McPhee didn't say anything for several long beats. Then he pushed the receipt and the Polaroid back across his desk, toward us. "It's a good story," he said, "but it's just that. A story. It's all circumstantial. You've got no hard evidence."

"But what about the receipt? The Polaroid?" I said.

"I can't arrest somebody on such flimsy evidence," he said.

"But—"

"When Lieutenant Douglas comes in on Monday, I'll tell him what you told me."

"Monday will be too late!" I shouted. "Someone's going to get bumped off *tonight*!"

"Sorry, kids," said the lieutenant, putting the file back in his desk. "There's nothing I can do."

13

Next Stop, Murder

The fifth floor of Presbyterian Hospital wasn't exactly my favorite place in the world. If I never set foot in an oncology unit again, it'll be too soon. But I had to suck it up. We had to find out who was next on Meredith's list.

Luckily, Brini Thompson was on duty at the nurses' station.

"Brini, you have to help us," Mackenzie said. "We think the Phantom killer is going to strike again tonight."

"Omigod!" Brini said, going pale. "Don't scare me, honey! I'm terrified enough as it is. The whole hospital is in a state of panic."

"But with your help, we can stop the killer," I said.

Brini took a deep breath, then exhaled. "Okay. I'm calm."

"Last time we were here, you told us about James Nichols," Mackenzie said.

"That's right," said Brini. "Omigod! Don't tell me *he's* the psycho killer!"

"No, he's not," I said. "A psycho, maybe, but not a killer. Do you remember a woman named Meredith Claiborne?"

"Sure. That was poor old Mrs. Claiborne's daughter." Brini looked indignant. "Accused us of killing her mother. Sued the hospital, you know."

"I know," Mackenzie said. "After her mother died, she went off the deep end. We think she's the killer."

"Omigod!" Brini exclaimed.

"Is there anybody on the floor who treated Mrs. Claiborne and who also takes the Eighty-sixth Street crosstown bus?" I asked.

"*I* used to!" she said, going pale. "But with all these murders, my fiancé, Donald, asked me not to anymore. So I've been walking. He's so sweet."

"Do you know of anyone here on staff who's still riding the bus?" Mackenzie asked.

Brini scrunched up her face. "Let me see. . . . Yeah, I think Mr. Strather. I used to see him on it every now and then. As far as I know, he still takes it."

"Mr. Strather?" I asked.

"Gil Strather. The pharmacist on the floor. Meredith got mad at him when he wouldn't give her a higher dosage of painkillers than what was prescribed by the doctors for her mother. Of course, it *was* enough painkillers. Just not enough to suit Miss Know-it-all."

"Where's Mr. Strather now?" I asked.

Brini looked at her watch. "Seven o'clock. His shift

just ended." She looked up, horrified. "He's probably on the way home right now. On the bus!"

As soon as we heard that, we made like Elvis and left the building. We charged down the sidewalk, dodging pedestrians, leaping over a panhandler sprawled across the pavement, jayrunning through a DON'T WALK sign, to the corner of Broadway. We were on Ninety-eighth Street when the bus, heading downtown, passed us.

"Come on, Mac!" I yelled. "This is it!" We flat-out sprinted the last two blocks, reaching the bus just before it pulled away from the curb.

"You kids sure wanted to catch this bus," the driver said as we ran our MetroCards through the meter.

Too winded to answer, we just collapsed into the first available seats. As we turned left crosstown onto Eighty-sixth Street, I said to Mackenzie, "It just occurred to me. We don't know what Strather looks like."

"That must be him over there," she said, nodding at a guy in a right-hand seat about halfway toward the back. He was wearing a white lab coat with PRESBYTERIAN HOSPITAL stenciled over the pocket.

"Let's go sit behind him," I suggested, "so we can keep a better eye on him."

"Okay. There's no way Meredith'll be able to get to him with us sitting right there."

We got up and walked toward the back of the bus. Plopping down in the seat behind Strather, I whispered to Mackenzie, "Now we wait—and watch."

At the Central Park West stop, the last one before the long leg east through the park, a crowd of people got on. The bus was suddenly so full that people were standing in the aisle. I peered through the forest of legs, coats, newspapers, and bags, looking for anyone who could be Meredith Claiborne, a.k.a. the Phantom of Eighty-sixth Street.

"Look," I whispered. "Over there." I pointed between the tall skinny guy in a jogging suit and the mohawked teenager playing with a Game Boy who were standing directly in front of us. Behind them, within an arm's length of Strather, stood a hunched-over figure in a long gray overcoat. Underneath the coat the person was wearing a sweatshirt, with the hood pulled up over the head.

"Is it a man or a woman?" I asked.

"Can't tell," Mackenzie whispered.

The bus lurched. The hooded figure took a half step, and I caught a brief glimpse of the person's face—it was a man's.

"It's not her," I said.

Mackenzie peered around. "What about her?" She pointed at the back of another person in the aisle whose face we couldn't see.

"Definitely a woman," I said, judging from the stockings and pumps. "But is it Meredith?"

The woman made a motion toward Strather. I tensed up, getting ready to spring. But all she did was push the signal over the window to let the driver know she wanted to get out at the next stop. I saw enough of her face to see that she wasn't Meredith.

"Nope," I whispered.

The bus slowed to a halt, at the stop midway through the park. There was shuffling and muttered *Excuse me*'s and *Coming through*s as the lady who'd pulled the cord tried to squeeze through the crowd and exit out the back.

"It's going to happen soon," I muttered. "I can feel it."

"Me too. My head's tingling like crazy. She's here somewhere. We've got to flush her out."

"But how?"

Suddenly I had an idea. I took out my cell phone. "Mac, do you still have Meredith's card?" I whispered. "What's her beeper number?"

"Why—?" Then she caught on. She rummaged through her messenger bag and read the number off to me. I punched it in.

Diddle-um, diddle-um, diddle-um-dum-dum! The *William Tell* Overture sounded dimly over the grinding of the engine and human sounds of the crowded bus.

"Did you hear it? Where's it coming from?" I looked around frantically.

"I don't know! It almost sounded like it was coming from—"

"Outside!" I shouted. I leaped forward and grabbed Strather, pushing him across down in his seat, just as the window next to us exploded in a shower of glass. Screams. People ducking, rushing for the back exit, climbing over each other to get out.

"Mac, are you okay?" I shouted.

"Fine," she yelled. "You?"

"Never better!" Realizing I still had Strather's collar gripped in my hands, and was sprawled half over him facedown in the aisle, I rolled him over. He looked completely bewildered, as well as terrified. "You okay?"

He nodded, slack-jawed.

"Great." I dropped him and jumped to my feet. "Mac, let's go!"

"Way ahead of you!" she called back, halfway out the bus's door.

In moments I'd bull-rushed my way through the crowd and joined Mackenzie on the sidewalk next to the bus. A total of maybe fifteen seconds had elapsed since the bus window had been shot out.

"Over there!" I shouted, pointing to the north side of the road.

In the shadows, a figure dropped a rifle and ran into the darkness of the park.

"After her!" Mackenzie yelled, and took off across the street.

14

Dawn

I dashed after Mackenzie. "Where'd she go?" I yelled.

"Over there!" came a voice to our left.

It was Officer Jamison, from the police kiosk on the south side of the street, waving a flashlight and sprinting toward the path that leads to the reservoir. He moved pretty fast for a chunky guy. We ran after him, following the beam of his flashlight up the pitch-black trail. Jamison was about a hundred yards in front of us on the trail when I grabbed Mackenzie's arm and whispered, "Mac! Stop!"

She froze. "What?"

I dragged her into the bushes by the side of the trail.

"Let's wait here," I murmured. "I'll bet anything Meredith ducks into the bushes, waits for Jamison to run past, then doubles back."

We waited in silence for several seconds. Very far away, on the west side of the park, sirens sounded. More cops were on the way.

Footsteps on the gravel path, coming from the direction Officer Jamison had run down. Walking briskly, but not running. Whoever it was was trying not to draw anyone's attention. In the dim light I could see it was Meredith Claiborne.

"Get her!" I cried, and we both leaped out into the path. Mackenzie drove her shoulder into Meredith's midsection, and I hit her high, knocking the wind right out of her. The three of us hit the path with a heavy thud, Mackenzie and me on top, Meredith beneath us.

It didn't take much effort after that to wrestle her into a secure hold.

"Officer Jamison!" Mackenzie yelled into the darkness. "Back here!"

In seconds his flashlight beam appeared on the path, heading in our direction. Meredith struggled to get away, screeching like a banshee, but I had her arm wrenched up behind her back. She wasn't going anywhere.

"The game's up, Meredith," I said. "You won't be killing anybody else."

Officer Jamison slapped the handcuffs on Meredith and hauled her to a squad car, and that was the last we saw of her.

We caught a ride with some other cops to the precinct house. Half an hour later, Lieutenant Douglas showed up. He wanted to take our official statement personally, so we recounted it one more time.

"Meredith must have followed us to the hospital on the night we nearly got gamma-rayed to death," I said.

"She knew how to operate the machine from all the months of taking her mom in for treatments."

"Seeing her mother suffer and die made something in her snap," said Mackenzie. "It's sad, really."

"So you believe Corbin and Nichols had nothing to do with the murders?" Lieutenant Douglas asked.

"That's right," I said. "Oh, Corbin's a thief, and he was angry enough about being fired that he sent threatening e-mails to the hospital. But his bark is worse than his bite."

"From what we've seen and heard, Nichols definitely has a bite to go with his bark," Mackenzie said. "But he hasn't killed anyone—at least not yet."

"Okay," said Lieutenant Douglas. "That about wraps things up. I want to thank you for your good work on the case. You saved a life tonight."

He held out his hand, and we shook.

By now it was past four in the morning. Mackenzie's parents came to get us. It was almost dawn by the time we made it back to the Riggses' brownstone.

"I am totally. Ragged. Out," I said, collapsing into the couch. I yawned and closed my eyes.

"Don't go to sleep yet, P.C.," Mac said. "Mom's making us scrambled eggs, and it's your duty to eat some."

I roused myself. "Actually, I could do with some food. My stomach's growling."

We took our plates to Mackenzie's room and sat cross-legged on the floor. Nothing tastes better than scrambled eggs in the morning when you've stayed up all night.

"It is sad about Meredith, you know," Mackenzie said. "I mean, at one level she was a monster—a cold-blooded killer who showed her victims no mercy. On another level, she's just a brokenhearted little girl who couldn't accept that her mother had died."

"It's a hard thing to accept," I said. "Your mother dying, I mean. Life bites, then you look down and half your insides have been eaten away."

A pigeon landed on the windowsill and cooed softly, ruffled its feathers, and flew away.

Mackenzie hugged me. "The best part of your mom is still alive in you, you know, P.C."

I felt tears coming into my eyes, but this time, I didn't turn away. I didn't care if Mackenzie saw.

"If she could see you now, she'd be so proud of you," she said. "I know she would."

The pigeon streaked past the window, shooting up toward the sky in a flash of iridescent gray. I blinked and a tear fell. I scooped up the last bit of scrambled egg. It was warm and good.

AND DON'T MISS . . .